Th

The Battle For Beaver Lake

Geoffrey Malone

KNIGHT BOOKS

Hodder and Stoughton

First published by Knight Books 1994

10 9 8 7 6 5 4 3 2 1

A catalogue record for this title is available from
the British Library

ISBN 0 340 61207 X

Typeset by Phoenix Typesetting
Ilkley, West Yorkshire

Printed and bound in Great Britain by
Cox & Wyman Ltd, Reading, Berks.

Hodder and Stoughton Ltd
A Division of Hodder Headline plc
338 Euston Road
London NW1 3BH

To Jennifer

The Battle For Beaver Lake

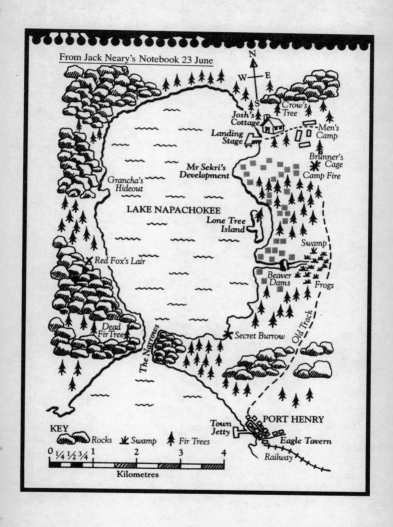

From Jack Neary's Notebook 23 June

N · W · E · S

Josh's Cottage
Crow's Tree
Landing Stage
Men's Camp
Brunner's Cage
Camp Fire
Mr Sekri's Development
Grancha's Hideout
LAKE NAPACHOKEE
Lone Tree Island
Swamp
Red Fox's Lair
Beaver Dams
Frogs
Dead Fir Tree
The Narrows
Secret Burrow
Old Track
PORT HENRY
Town Jetty
Eagle Tavern
Railway

KEY
🪨 Rocks   🌿 Swamp   🌲 Fir Trees

0 ¼ ½ ¾ 1   2   3   4
Kilometres

CHAPTER ONE

Brunner stood stock still. He knew he was being followed. He had known for the past ten minutes. Ever since he had scrambled down that last outcrop he had had this prickly sensation running up and down his spine. He sat back on his haunches, folded his large flat tail beneath him for balance and listened intently.

He was hidden where he was. Safe for the time being under the lower branches of a fir tree still weighed down with snow. The beaver put his head to one side to concentrate better.

At first he could hear nothing new, just the music of the northern night. The sound the air makes as it streams from place to place beneath the immensity of the heavens. A tinkling, hissing noise like a pine cone flicked over a sheet of newly-formed ice. A sky that seemed to stretch for ever, dwarfing the mountains to the west and north.

An owl was hunting. It was hungry and angry at having caught nothing all night. Brunner followed its flight as it beat backwards and forwards a little way in front of him. Then it was gone. Beside him, a branch shivered and shed a weight of snow.

Reassured by the silence, he scraped away the snow where it had frozen under the webs of his hind feet. It was packed into hard ridges that made walking awkward and uncomfortable. The heat of his body melted the snow at first but it had quickly refrozen. For the tenth time that night he cleared the icy mush away. He noticed one of the pads was bleeding, worn raw after five nights' travelling.

It was hard work for a beaver walking through soft snow like this. The spring thaw was well advanced and though there was still a frost at night, the mid-April sun grew stronger and shone later with each passing day.

Everywhere, winter was in full retreat. On each lake, the ice floes were breaking up and shrinking. Every day they became more slushy as they melted back into the water. Along the shorelines, black earth appeared and the fir trees slid the last remnants of snow off their branches.

Only here on the higher ground was the snow still deep. But it was old snow, heavy with water and too tired to last much longer. It was exhausting work pushing a path through it and every few steps Brunner would sink into it up to his shoulders. The temptation to stay where he was and simply curl up and sleep was becoming insistent but that way led to certain death. He needed to reach the safety of the water.

Brunner decided to rest at the next lake. He would wait to get his breath back before struggling on any further. He was in very poor condition and it was becoming a great effort to keep going.

He had spent a wretched winter holed up in a disused burrow on his own, close to a thriving colony of beavers who had rejected him and driven him away. He had first caught their musky scent as he had fled in blind panic from the men who had killed his parents that terrible time, the previous November.

He and the younger beavers had waited all night for their parents to return from a feeding trip. Brunner, as the biggest and strongest had been left in charge. At first they groomed themselves then played, tussling over pieces of bark and broken twigs. Later, they grew restless, then bored, and increasingly hungry. Brunner twice had to drag his brother back from slipping out of the lodge's underwater entrance in defiance of the parents' orders. Beavers live in tight family units with a very well defined social structure, so it took considerable courage on his part to swim out eventually to see what had happened.

The first thing he had seen after he cleared the entrance was a thick birch stake that had not been there before. Wrapped round the foot of it was a length of chain that disappeared into the gloom of the deeper water. Brunner had followed it. A couple of thrusts from his powerful hind legs and he noticed something below him lying on the muddy bottom. He dived towards it and found his mother with a front paw caught in a trap. She was dead – her mouth fully open. The weight of the trap had drowned her.

He surfaced, spluttering from the shock. The sudden splash alerted the men. They got to their feet and pointed at him. Almost at once he caught their scent; a sweet cloying taste that settled on the back of his tongue. They shouted and the beaver saw that one of them was holding a long, curved knife. There was blood on his hands and forearms.

Brunner dived in and swam underwater until his lungs felt they would burst. Only then did he surface and only for the briefest possible moment to draw breath. He swam without any idea where he was going. Hours later, it seemed, he was caught in a sudden powerful torrent. Swept sideways over a smooth lip of rock, he fell for what seemed an eternity into a deep pool beneath. It winded him so much, he let the river carry him along for the next mile. Then it opened out and slowed.

Later, he picked up the scent of beaver and found the lodge. It was a massive affair, close to nine feet high.

The mud packed between the branches of its sides and top already frozen solid. He dived down and found the entrance almost at once. Perhaps it was the suddenness of his appearance or more likely the smell of fear which clung to him, that terrified the occupants. With uncharacteristic savageness for his species, the oldest male went for him, striking down at his head with extended claws and narrowly missing Brunner's eye. The others set up a deafening hissing which prevented his pleas being heard.

He turned and bolted but there was no pursuit. He swam in aimless circles uttering the plaintive whines of babyhood. It wasn't until the chill of exhaustion spread through his body that he spotted the old burrow and gratefully crept in.

It had been a miserable time. He spent it shivering and aching with hunger. The winter had been hard and the ice had frozen to within two feet of the bottom of the river. He had barely enough time to cut down and store food before the first great blizzard struck. He worked frantically before this cutting all the branches from whatever aspen or alder trees he could find and then dragging them back to the burrow. Here he stored them securely in the riverbed as a larder against the bad weather to come.

Now, five long months later, Brunner was again on the move. He had no clear idea why he was venturing out into danger like this. Perhaps it was just instinct telling him to put as much distance as possible between himself and the trappers. He was at home gliding through the lakes and crossing the rivers he came to. It was the overland stretches which frightened him. Here he was ill at ease. His feet slipped and slithered in the snow, slowing him down.

All this time, he had been listening. He sniffed at the night air, testing the scents it carried. Silently he left the shadows and continued his journey. Tiny smears of blood from the raw patch on his foot made occasional stains in the snow behind him.

As he emerged from under the trees, he screwed up his eyes. The moonlight threaded a dazzling path between the trees. Almost blindly, Brunner hurried on, squinting into the white glare and tensing himself to recognise the first smell of water. He put his head down and trudged on.

A quarter of a mile behind, a lynx examined the trail the beaver had left. It snuffled over the tracks, pawing at them to uncover further information. It licked at the bloodstains, then followed at a slow bound.

The old alarm clock went off with a clatter. It shrilled with enthusiasm and did its best to slide off the chair on to the floor. Josh Gilpin extended a hand, found the clock and finally stilled the noise. From his basket by the door of the cottage, Ranger uttered a groan of protest. As always on these occasions, the dog lay perfectly still, willing the old man to drop off back to sleep. He had lived with Josh for ten years and still could not for the life of him fathom why his master wanted to leave a warm bed just to sit hunched up over a fishing line in a small boat, at dawn. It made no sense at all.

Ranger waited a while longer, then just as he was beginning to settle down again, he heard the unmistakable sound of the man groping for the flashlight he kept under the bed. Sure enough, it flicked on.

'Time to get up, old fellow,' Josh called, yawning. He pushed back the patched grey blankets and shuffled over to the kitchen table which stood in the middle of the floor. He fiddled with a box of matches and after a couple of attempts, the room was filled with light and the hiss of a pressure lamp.

Next Josh lit the tiny gas stove and put the kettle on. Ten minutes later, he was urging a reluctant Ranger outside.

'What's up then?' he asked, shutting the door behind them. 'You should have been with me in the old days on the railroad. Up at four every morning for nigh on forty years. Yes, Sir!'

Ranger ignored him. Josh always said that. It was part of the ritual. He smelt the early morning air without enthusiasm. It was dark, damp and miserable. He shook himself and followed the man down the short track that led to the jetty. In front of them, Lake Napachokee looked half asleep. He clambered into the boat, barked his shin on a thwart and gave a sharp yelp of pain.

Josh untied the painter, reached for the oars and shipped half a gallon of cold water over the dog's back. Furious, Ranger sulked in the bows, listening to the oars and Josh's breathing.

Later, as the grey of dawn picked out the shape of individual trees along the shoreline, Josh stopped rowing and started to busy himself with his rods. He worked with a quiet intensity and before long had flicked a long line out to where the first breeze of the day was ruffling the surface of the lake. He pushed a hand into the pocket of his coat and offered Ranger a biscuit.

'Wonder if we'll see those beavers this morning,' he said conversationally. 'Can't be that far from their dam, out here.'

Ranger treated the remark with the contempt it deserved. He couldn't care less whether they saw them or not. He crunched open the biscuit and found, too late, it was charcoal flavoured. It was going to be one of those days.

* * *

Barely half a mile from where Josh was fishing, an elderly beaver was swimming up and down checking on the condition of the dam. This was old Nathan, who had lived here, close to where the river flowed into Lake Napachokee, for almost twelve years. He was old for a beaver in the wild and his muzzle was white with age.

He trod water and looked along the length of the dam wall to the far bank some thirty yards away. He could see no obvious change in its shape, though he knew the pressure on it was growing by the hour. He measured the water level against a prominent boulder. There was no doubt – it had risen a good body's width since this time yesterday. He could feel the increased pressure of the current on his flanks, pushing him into the face of the dam. By tomorrow, it would be that much higher again, as the spring thaw filled the streams with water from the melting ice fields high up in the mountains.

At surface level, there didn't appear to be too much wrong with the structure. The four of them, Mataama and her twins Chipwe and Petwa together with Nathan himself, spent a great deal of time the previous autumn preparing the dam for the winter ahead. It had been the twins' first lessons in dam building and they had set to it with enthusiasm. They had learnt how to cut branches into similar sizes and how to drag them back through the water. They had been shown how to plaster the inside walls of the two dams with mud. They packed gaps with stones and knew that the best way to carry heavy objects was wedged between front paws and chin. But they were young and inexperienced.

Nathan dived down to see what was happening underwater. He found a branch that was being tugged out of position by the strength of the flow. He grasped the top of it with his front paws and then held it firmly between his two massive front teeth. He gave a series of tugs and

15

at last managed to drag it clear. He scrambled up on top of the dam and pushed the branch back down. He kept pushing it until it had wedged in place. By this time, the dawn was well advanced and Nathan knew it had taken him far too long to do that simple repair.

The trouble was, he was getting old and his front paws were swollen with arthritis. He could no longer flex his fingers easily. They were becoming clumsy and ached most of the time he was awake. He knew he wouldn't be much use to Mataama and her young if the river burst through the dams. If they couldn't repair them, then the lodge would be left high and dry – open to attack from any predator who came along.

Gloomily he sank into the quieter waters between the dams and headed for the lodge. It was time to sleep.

Death comes suddenly in the wild. Whether it is the explosive pounce of a hawk or the shocking speed of a water snake striking at a frog, the victim has little indication of what is to come. Brunner had only himself to blame. The going was easier now, the ground sloping steeply down to a lake. The smell of water was everywhere. The trees were aspen and alder which meant food at last. He was absorbed in his surroundings when the lynx attacked.

It came at him from the higher ground to his right and hit the beaver just below the shoulder. The lynx was over-confident. It had sensed that Brunner was ill at ease in the snow and was having problems seeing. It had watched the beaver blunder into snow drifts which any land-based animal would have known how to avoid. Then there was the way it kept biting its paw and the limp it was developing.

The lynx chose his place well. It raced ahead and lay in wait in a small stand of trees. It lay motionless until

16

Brunner had passed below then came at him in great silent bounds. But this impatience lost it the advantage.

Instead of throwing the beaver off balance by going for its throat, the lynx bit down and sank its teeth into the thickness of Brunner's pelt. Brunner slewed to one side then fell heavily on his shoulder. For a split second, he could not think what was happening. He slid over the snow, his legs kicking frantically to regain his balance, his chin tucked down to protect his throat. Above him, the lynx was shaking its jaws from side to side, trying to bite down through the fur to the soft skin underneath.

Its back claws slashed at Brunner's stomach, ripping the fur out in tufts, and its breath was sour on his muzzle. Brunner was paralysed with fright. His limbs seemed to have turned to water and the powerful muscles in his hind legs hung loose and heavy. There was a roaring in his ears like some enormous waterfall. He felt he was drowning.

The weight of the lynx was pushing him deeper into the snow, making escape more impossible with every second that passed. He was being forced into an ice coffin. Soon he would be unable to move. The lynx's teeth raked across Brunner's nose and the pain was so intense, it broke the terror that kept him helpless.

His fear turned to rage and a surge of energy enabled him to get both hind feet under the lynx and, in one almighty heave, catapult it off to one side.

Brunner struggled to his feet gasping for air and only just in time to meet the other's next charge. He staggered back under the impact and went over again. The snow was slushy and heavy. Brunner knew he couldn't keep up the fight for much longer. The fury of the attack was draining his strength. He faltered and shut his eyes to keep out the lynx's fierce grin. But still he fought.

They rolled over and over, snarling and struggling for advantage until, almost in slow motion, they slid off the bank and fell four feet into the water below. The lynx broke off and churned the water with its paws. It headed back to the shore screeching its shock and frustration in a series of high pitched cries.

From the lake, Brunner watched it disappear into the scrub while he swam in a slow circle to get his breath back, letting the coldness of the water soothe the pain that ran through him. The lake felt welcoming and familiar and gradually reassured him that out here no animal could harm him. The shivering stopped as his confidence returned. In front of him the shoreline was a dark blur. He could smell snow flurries on the wind. Brunner blew a stream of bubbles and slipped under the surface.

CHAPTER TWO

At about the same time as Josh was frying the two
lake trout he had caught for breakfast, a telephone rang
in the plush offices of Parker Properties Incorporated,
one thousand miles to the south.

'It's your lawyer, sir,' said the secretary. 'He's calling
from the land auction. Would you like to talk to him or
shall I get him to call back later?'

'Put him through at once,' Mr Sekri snapped.

He drummed impatient fingers on the marble top of his
desk and stared at a bronze bust of himself that stood on
an elaborate Louis XVI stand in a far corner of the room.
This new woman was hopeless, he thought. She had no
concept of urgency. No feel for the business. Everyone
knew that for a big time property developer like himself,
even a couple of minutes delay could be fatal and you
could lose out on some great business opportunity. No,
she'd have to go, that very day. After six o'clock though.
May as well get a day's work out of her first.

Mr Sekri was a small man, who was described by
the newspapers as an entrepreneur. He had one god –
making money. Years ago he had learnt the value of
never showing outward emotion. He had a gambler's
instinct for weighing up chances and taking calculated
risks. An uncle, recognising his innate business skills,
had left him a small carpentry business. Mr Sekri had
developed it into a commercial empire that now employed over 20,000 people. He was heartless, ruthless
and fawned over by politicians.

Right now, he had got wind of a nice little piece of property up in the Northlands which, if properly handled, would be a real money spinner. It was on a lake and would make a perfect place to develop an exclusive wildlife and outdoor sports resort. Mr Sekri would develop the place and sell it on to some leisure company in time for summer and make a fat profit into the bargain. He had done his sums. This place was perfect and it was coming up at a public auction that morning.

'That you, Burns?' he rasped after the connection was made. 'What's the score?'

From the other end of the phone the lawyer told him. Mr Sekri made notes: '2,000 acres ... ten miles from airstrip at Port Henry ... So, what's the catch?' he asked.

'There's a restrictive covenant,' the lawyer explained, 'tucked away in the land title deeds.'

'Tell me more,' Mr Sekri ordered.

'Well,' said the other man, 'seems like the city fathers who owned the land back in 1895 sold it to the railway company but stipulated that any railroad worker who built a permanent dwelling and lived there for five years, would be entitled to stay there at a peppercorn rent. They wanted to encourage settlement there, I believe.'

'So?' Mr Sekri challenged.

'The folks who took up the offer could build a cottage and have two hundred acres of land surrounding their house, in perpetuity,' Burns enlarged.

'And I've bought the land, so what's the problem?' Mr Sekri demanded.

'What it means,' the lawyer told him, 'is that although you may own the land, there is no legal way you can get rid of this man Gilpin. Trouble is, he's sitting on the best piece of land.'

Mr Sekri considered this in silence.

Burns went on: 'Gilpin is the great grandson of the original tenant and still lives in the original house. He is therefore the legal owner of that house, some of Lake Napachokee and most of the lakeshore you need, I'm afraid.'

There was a further silence.

'As you know,' Burns added in a rather unctuous voice, 'that restriction applies as much today as it did then. In law, there's no way we can get round it, I'm afraid.'

'Let's get this straight,' Mr Sekri said slowly. 'There's just this one house belonging to this Gilpin guy? So how do we get him out?'

The lawyer cleared his throat with a little cough. 'Well,' he said, 'the local land registry in Port Henry was destroyed by fire in the summer of '39. Looks like this whole thing could have all fallen through the cracks so far as anyone up there will ever remember.'

'And if we can't buy off a couple of local hayseed councillors, if needs be, we shouldn't be in this business,' Mr Sekri said with relish.

'So do I buy?' Burns asked.

Mr Sekri thought hard for a while then a faint shadow of a smile appeared for an instant. 'Go for it!' he ordered. 'I'll have my people move on it right away. By the time the machines have flattened the place, it'll be too late.'

He rang off and pressed the intercom button. 'Get me Bourassa,' he snapped.

In the main chamber of the lodge, Mataama and the twins were feeding. The three of them sat on dry ground near the underwater entrance, stripping bark from the branches Chipwe and Petwa had towed back from the swamp earlier that day. They nibbled at the sappy-flavoured aspens, rotating them between their fingers like so many corn cobs.

As they did so, they reviewed the day's events. There had been two scares with the dam when the river had threatened to break through. The sound of flowing water is one no beaver can resist investigating. It means there is a hole in the dam demanding instant action. They had all worked hard repositioning branches and threading new ones into the fabric to staunch the flow.

To old Nathan's secret relief, the young beavers had performed well. Now, he lay sound asleep, too tired even to eat with them.

Between Mataama and her two yearlings, there was a comfortable acceptance of one another. There was hardly any need to talk as they could sense each other's concerns and thoughts by instinct. The common bond of family added a further layer of mutual understanding to this silent intimacy. Their worries about the dam were assessed and anticipated even while they sat, squirrel-like, munching tender pieces of bark.

When they had finished, Mataama groomed them in turn, taking care to rub the body oil each beaver secretes deep down into the roots of their fur. This would keep their pelts unmatted and water repellant. It would also act as insulation against the coldness of the water. Both twins were perfectly able to do this for themselves but as Chipwe said, if it made their mother happy, then why not?

After this, they set to cleaning the main living chamber of sticks, pieces of bark and pebbles. This took a little time. Beavers are fastidious creatures and the chamber was a large one, over three yards in diameter. Next they tidied the area where they all slept. If Mataama had had a mate, the young beavers would have made their own quarters elsewhere inside the lodge.

When all was finished, Mataama yawned a couple of times and curled up close to Nathan. Chipwe and Petwa quietly slipped into the water and swam down the steep tunnel that led to the river and the great world outside.

Up on top, the day had dawned. Already there was a warmth in the sun that stirred memories of hot, lazy days and cool, shady places to rest. The air was clear and for an animal, it carried a perfect feast of scents and smells.

Like all animals, beavers depend to a huge degree on instinct and the most important part of that is a highly developed sense of self-preservation. It was one thing to fool around at the bottom of a well-built beaver lodge but out here, in the sunshine, there was only survival. So it was that the two of them at first only let their eyes and nostrils break the surface. They waited, and listened, and absorbed the scents, reconciling what was out there with their experience and memory. For several minutes they stayed like this, steadying themselves with a gentle paddle from their powerful tails. Ahead of them, a succession of lake trout came gleaming to the surface, poking their heads out to see if the early season's flies had arrived before flicking back downwards in one easy movement.

There was a distinct human smell in the air that morning. That was the man Josh, who lived on the shores of Lake Napachokee with his dog, Ranger. Chipwe and Petwa quite liked Josh. He would often come round in his boat late in the afternoon and talk to them, not far from the lower dam where the beavers' river flowed into the lake. Josh would let his boat drift in the current in a long, lazy circle while he fished. The beavers would watch him and Josh would sit there and talk to them. He told them his name and that he was a very old animal.

Petwa thought he was probably as old as Nathan. And Chipwe said what a pity they couldn't swap him.

He didn't seem to mind if they played round his boat even though this meant scaring away the fish. They didn't understand all he said, but they were proud of 'their' human. Ranger was not impressed in the least. He had once leapt into the lake to chase them away but it hadn't taken the beavers long to realise he was no match for them. So they would swim in very close to where Ranger sat in the bows and hurl taunts at him. Ranger just looked bored and ignored them.

They no longer told the older beavers about their friendship with the man. The first time it had happened last summer, they had been beside themselves with excitement and had raced back to the lodge. Nathan was so angry that he had hissed with rage. He hated all men. Mataama had made them promise never to go anywhere near Josh and the dog again. But of course, they had.

Once, in an act of huge daring, Chipwe and Petwa had actually crept ashore and investigated Josh's cottage. It was extraordinary. A vast, gloomy chamber that stretched away on all sides. It was stuffed with huge things they had never seen before. Petwa had put a pine cone in Ranger's bed, but after this their nerve broke. The crows, who gathered in the trees nearby, were scandalised at their behaviour and threatened to tell. They had had some difficulty getting Ranger's strong dog smell out of their pelts before they returned to the lodge but in the end, they were never discovered.

They could smell strong cooking smells from the old man's cottage and they could also hear Ranger barking away at the squirrels. Elsewhere, they picked up the scent of the red fox which had a den in a cave in the rocks on the far side of the lake. Although there wasn't much contact between beavers and foxes, like all the lake dwellers Chipwe and Petwa were suspicious of them.

On this morning, however, they decided there was nothing to cause any alarm so they swam to the nearest bank and padded ashore. Petwa saw that the mud was already dry where they had constructed a wonderful ice-slide a couple of weeks ago when there was still thick ice over most of the water.

They had sat on their tails and in a state of high old excitement had gone whizzing down the almost vertical slope and far out on to the ice. They had intended to do it again the next day but then the last blizzard of the winter came howling out of the North and dumped three foot of snow over everything. It was about this time that they heard a wolf pack in the vicinity and no one left the lodge, until they heard the ice starting to break up above them.

This morning, Chipwe and Petwa studied the upper dam for some time in silence. They stared at the water where it lapped against the structure, noting its force and flow, looking for faster moving eddies or broken streams of water that would mean there was further damage to the internal fabric.

The dam creaked and gave an occasional wheeze from deep down below the surface where the pressure was remorseless. The beavers scrambled up and ran along its length from bank to bank. They could feel the vibrations of the water's struggle through their paws and it alarmed them.

'Feels like a living thing,' said Chipwe worriedly. 'As if it's moving around down there.'

'Should we warn old Nathan?' Petwa asked.

Chipwe listened intently, twitching his ears in concentration. Then he gave a shrug. 'You heard what he told Mataama,' he replied. 'It could go at any time.'

'Let's see how much fuller the swamp is overnight,' suggested Petwa. 'He'll want to know that as soon as he wakes.'

Above the dam was the swamp. This had been formed countless years ago from the silt the river deposited after one of Grandpa Nathan's ancestors had originally built the dams and the family lodge. Now, it stretched back for a good hundred yards into the surrounding forest and was deep under water. In summer, it was the home of the frogs, who spent the evenings quarrelling with one another and then throwing enormous parties to make up. Old Nathan hated the frogs. In his opinion, they encouraged water snakes which were no addition to anyone's environment.

Overhead, above the icy waters of the river, the sun grew hotter. The sky became a darker shade of blue and in the forest and along the edges of Lake Napachokee, countless numbers of insects woke up and began scurrying here, there and everywhere with that fixed intensity that only ants, beetles and some school teachers have.

Josh was starting the outboard engine of his boat. He adjusted the fuel supply, wrapped the cord around the flywheel and gave a short, hard pull. The engine caught second time and was soon revving in impatience to be off. He undid the painter and pushed them away from the small, wooden jetty that lay fifty yards below the cottage. He pushed the tiller over and Ranger standing up in the bows, dug his nails in to counter the heel of the boat. He had once absent-mindedly forgotten to do this and still cringed with embarrassment at the memory of Josh's laughter when he all but slid overboard. Behind them, a pair of crows hopped over the tiny front lawn.

Josh was in his usual good mood. Although something of a recluse, he enjoyed his weekly trips to the little town. He was heading for Port Henry, the only human settlement in a hundred miles. Here, he would stop and chat to a great many people. He would go to the post office and check to see if there was any mail. When there was, it was usually the newsletter from his old railroad association. Then he'd go and have one beer at the Eagle Tavern at the end of Main Street. Ranger wasn't too keen on the Tavern. It was smoky and that made his eyes water. He didn't care much for the smells either. As a further drawback, the biggest cat he had ever seen lived there. It was a battle scarred tom who sneered at him. Ranger ignored him and deliberately looked in some other direction. The only trouble was the cat knew this and with the usual perversity of its kind, would saunter along the bench Josh sat on and rub itself up against the old human.

While Josh patted him and tickled him under the chin, the cat would mock Ranger with huge yellow eyes and sheath and unsheath its claws right in front of him. Of course the man did not realise what was going on and was in fact quite proud of the fuss the cat made of him.

Ranger sighed. Josh could be so dumb at times. However, there was no doubt about it. Josh was also one of the happiest animals for miles.

He sang snatches of songs; laughed and called witticisms to the dog, who was by now sitting somewhat shame-facedly staring out from the bows. All this howling from back aft was not doing his master nor, by association, himself any good. He could imagine the gossip and the giggles from such appalling creatures as the crows. Ranger sat looking noble and devoted to his heavy human responsibility and pretended the engine noise drowned everything.

Ranger was very fond of Josh. For years, the two of them had got along famously. His human shunned company of his own sort. Over the years, the only visitors they had entertained had been the occasional fur trapper and, more recently, garishly dressed and self-proclaimed friends of nature from the big city in the South. They had been fed and sent on their way soon after breakfast.

In the last couple of weeks, however, a shadow had been cast across Ranger's trips to Port Henry. This took the form of a new human female assistant at Ranger's favourite place – Mason's General Stores. For years there had only been jovial Mr Mason himself, who always had a bone put aside for Ranger or at the very least, a handful of biscuits. Now this woman, this wretched human, had refused to let him into the store. She insisted he had to be tied to a post outside like some untrained puppy. It was all to do with hygiene, she explained in a humourless tone. Josh, to his shame, had gone along with her request.

In their different moods, the two of them noted the miles slipping past. They looked out for the dead fir tree that marked the entrance to the narrow channel which led through to the bigger lake beyond. It was a wild, gloomy place and Ranger always shivered as they entered it. Rock walls towered above them and the waves would splash against the sides sending sudden showers of spray over the bows. Then, they were through and the noise of rushing water and the boom of the engine would recede, as they headed out into the lake opening up in front of them.

Soon, Port Henry could be seen on the left hand shore. It was a neat little place not dissimilar from a score of other outposts in the North. Most of its buildings were single-storey cabins, though there were a few grand town houses where the oldest families lived. There was one large street, aptly named 'Main Street' by a literal-minded mayor at the turn of the century, which boasted a number of impressive wooden buildings. These included the courthouse, the bank, the hospital and the offices of the local newspaper. At the other end of town, the railway station dozed in the sunshine. A diesel switching engine stood on the solitary track and hummed to itself. Its driver munched a sandwich and read the local paper.

Josh cut the engine and the boat touched the wooden pier with the smallest of sighs. Whatever else he did nowadays to embarrass him, Ranger decided Josh had lost none of his practical skills. A friendly human took the painter and whipped it round a bollard, making them fast. Ranger was heaved up level with the deck planking and the two of them went ashore.

Mason's General Store was located close to the end of the pier, across long defunct railway lines that bore testimony to the town's former past as a trading station and an earlier optimism for its future. It had belonged to the Hudson Bay Company, but that was way back when even Josh was young. In those days, the Indians and the trappers had brought in sledge loads of winter furs – fox, mink, sable, beaver and raccoon. They had taken bales of clothing, cooking pots and food, tobacco and whisky in exchange. There was one particular corner of the store which fascinated Ranger, where all those faint memories of the past still lingered. He ran ahead.

'Sorry old chap!' Josh said patting him and making him sit outside. The store was cool and dark and it smelt as always of fresh coffee and leather.

Ranger gave an expressive sigh and scratched himself. He slumped down on the wooden boardwalk and gloomily rested his chin on his front paws. A pick-up truck rattled past and the dog wrinkled his nose at the smell of exhaust. A cloud of fine dust tickled his nostrils. Already the spring thaw was drying into sand.

A couple of humans walked by and one of them recognised him. Ranger opened an eye but did not lift his head. He couldn't help his tail twitching. He lay there looking as thoroughly bored as only a dog can.

A fly buzzed at his face and settled on his nose. Ranger sneezed and swatted at it. The fly flew away to bother someone else. Ranger fell back into a doze until the sound of Josh's voice brought him to his feet. It was not so much the noise he made but the tone of voice the man was using.

Josh came into the sunshine clutching a newspaper in one hand. Ranger was shocked at the expression on his face. Josh was clearly upset. What had happened? Ranger growled, then ran alongside the man, looking up at him in great concern all the way back to the boat. Every now and then he would jump up at Josh to try and reassure him. As they reached the quay, Ranger began to bark, demanding to know what had shocked the man so much.

Josh got Ranger back in the boat and threw the newspaper down after him. It landed on a thwart and its banner headline proclaimed:

LAKE NAPACHOKEE ACQUIRED FOR GIGANTIC HOLIDAY DEVELOPMENT

Josh cast off and almost fell over Ranger in so doing. He started the engine, opened the throttle wide and the boat made a tight, banking turn. The water rushed up along the bow and Ranger looked back in surprise. Josh was looking angry, mighty angry. He was crying!

There were tears, real tears on his cheeks. He wiped his eyes with the back of his hand.

He shouted at Ranger, who struggled to hear what he was saying. 'Don't you see, if this thing goes through it'll mean the end of everything good; everything we've believed in. How are we going to stop it? How?' He started to cry again. This time he didn't even bother trying to hide his feelings. Ranger was frightened. There was some big threat coming. He could feel it. Well, he'd be ready for it, whatever it was. He clambered back to lick Josh's hand. The bows tilted higher as the speed increased and Ranger went sprawling.

At the end of the same day, long after the sun had set in the cool greyness of the evening, Brunner found a place for the night. It was a tiny island that stuck out by itself in the middle of a lake.

The beaver scrambled up its smooth sides and lay for a while on a flat slab of rock, his flanks heaving and his eyes closed. Later, Brunner explored the island. He found a place to sleep in a hollow deep in the roots of a dead fir tree. Old pine needles had blown in here during the winter storms and they were dry and smelt of better times.

He could find no traces of any other animals save for the droppings of generations of birds that lay encrusted on the rocks all around. He sat upright on his haunches and made as best a meal as he could of the low, shrubby bushes he found growing in sheltered places. The wood tasted sour and unsatisfying.

Later he groomed himself, licking delicately at the black gashes in his shoulder. His rough tongue cleaned away the old blood until he could feel the sting of raw flesh. He stopped then and instead puffed out his fur for greater warmth and settled down to sleep with a throaty little cry of relief. His whole body ached and his ribs were bruised and tender from the lynx's attack. He knew he would be stiff in the dawn.

Tomorrow he would slip back into the black waters of the lake and continue his quest for acceptance. Soon he would meet his own kind again, of that he was certain. How they would respond to him did not concern him. That was a hypothetical question compared to his immediate concern for self-preservation.

He burrowed into the pine leaves and turned round several times, loosening them so that they half covered him. He listened for a little longer but was reassured by the sound of water slapping at the rocks below. Satisfied, he fell into a dreamless sleep.

CHAPTER THREE

The helicopter came the following afternoon. Chipwe and Petwa were flicking pine cones at one another when Chipwe stopped and sat up. He peered at the sky, ignoring Petwa's protests.

'Listen,' he called. 'What's that?'

Petwa's tail whipped another cone past him. 'Hey! Don't stop. That's not fair,' he cried.

Chipwe waved him to silence. 'Listen!' he hissed. 'Can't you hear it?'

They listened. For a long moment there was nothing to hear, just a very unusual silence, which had to mean that other animals were listening too. There was something strange out there. They were both aware of that. An odd noise they had never heard before, almost as if someone was slapping a heavy tail on thin ice. It wasn't an echo exactly because it was too aggressive for that. It was alive, not an imitation. Besides, it was quite distinct and getting louder and still this same rhythmical, slapping sound. As far as they could judge, it was coming from south of the lake. They began to feel uneasy.

A flight of ducks exploded out of the reed beds and flew fast up the lake towards the beavers. They quacked in alarm and went over very low. The noise was increasing to a loud roar. Chipwe and Petwa moved closer together, tensed to dive, but still half-rooted to the spot in fascination. The noise now seemed to fill the lake. Whatever it was had to be hiding behind the fir trees. Perhaps it was watching them, waiting to pounce. And then an angry, bellowing, red creature leapt up high into the sky like some gigantic dragonfly and swooped down, heading straight for them.

They dived, their heavy flat tails smacking the water in a warning that was drowned by the snarl of the approaching helicopter. They swam in pure fright down to the bottom of the lake and waited there for a good eight minutes before slowly letting their bodies rise to take the most cautious of breaths. It was the longest dive Chipwe and Petwa had ever done.

Even before they broke surface, they could sense the presence of the newcomer creature. The surrounding water vibrated with the noise it made. It felt as if someone had your head in his hands and was shaking it from side to side, Petwa thought. Chipwe looked around and was shocked to see the red creature hovering only fifty yards away. Its wings went thumping round, chasing each other and sending black furrows shooting across the surface of the water. He knew it had to belong to human beings.

'What is it?' Petwa shouted as he trod water alongside him.

Chipwe shook his head 'Well, it ain't good news and that's for sure.'

The red machine bellowed and began to pour out black smoke. It moved forward as if feeling its way. Perhaps it was blind, Chipwe thought. It crossed the shoreline close to the cottage and moved towards a patch of cleared land where Josh grew summer corn. Its voice became more raucous, debris whipped up from the ground and a wind from nowhere flew into the beavers' eyes. They dived again.

Big Brian Bourassa lived up to his name. He was a very large human. He had cropped hair, no neck and shoulders that stuck out on either side. His arms were covered in thick black hair and when he put his hands on his hips, most other men were happy to agree with him. He wore jeans, a plaid shirt and a baseball cap.

He sat beside the pilot waiting for the rotors to finish turning. He put a fresh matchstick in a corner of his mouth and proceeded to chew it. He had worked for Mr Sekri these past eight years on a range of developments. Most of them had been straightforward demolition and rebuilding jobs. Occasionally, there was one where the locals got it into their heads to make a fuss. Those were the best ones and the competition for the job of project manager for one of them was intense. The best one he had ever been involved with was building a golf course over some ground a bunch of Indians claimed was sacred. Mr Sekri had naturally seen to it that the local authorities were sympathetic and Bourassa and his men had sorted out the protesters in quick time. This one, up here in the North, didn't seem to be special in any sort of way. Bourassa wondered why anyone would want to pay good money just to come up to this god-forsaken neck of the woods for a couple of weeks holiday each year.

No, he thought, looking round from inside the helicopter, this place should be easy. Just this crazy old guy living in the cottage. He'd soon get rid of him when Mr Sekri gave the green light. Outside, the blades had come to a halt.

'OK, you guys. Let's get cracking!' he growled into the intercom. Bourassa clambered out into the shocked silence. He stood beside the door as the other three occupants squeezed past. They stretched cramped leg muscles and gazed at the lake and surrounding trees. Bourassa gave them a moment or two then swung into action.

'OK! OK! Let's get with it, eh? Let's unload. Get the tent

up. And put some food on.' He began hauling bundles from inside the cabin and tossing them at the others. 'Don't forget there are still wolves round here. So look smart.'

From the safety of their vantage point beneath the overhanging branches of a blue spruce tree, Chipwe and Petwa watched in amazement. They had never seen so many humans together in one place before. Their antics were confusing. First of all, the big man with the long arms went over to Josh's cottage and tried the door. Josh kept it locked these days against the raccoons, who were quite capable of turning the door knob and once inside, trashing the place. Bourassa had then walked round looking in the windows, pressing his face to the glass for a better squint inside. He returned to the front door, put his shoulder against it and heaved it open with a sudden, strong shove. The lock splintered and he strode in.

Whilst he was doing this, the others were putting up a tent on the grass above the lakeshore. Chipwe and Petwa were impressed with how little time it took to build what was clearly their equivalent of a lodge. Once it was up, the men lit a fire and boiled water from the lake in a pot. The big man returned eating something he had found in the cottage. Then he had made them unpack the wooden crates they had brought with them. In half an hour, they had assembled their equipment and strode up the hill behind the cottage. Here one of them held a coloured pole upright while another man bent over a strange, three legged object. He spent a lot of time lining it up on the pole. Later, the big man shouted to them that food was ready and took a drink from a shiny bottle. He did not offer it to anyone else.

Slowly, the other animals and birds got over their shock and went about their business more or less as usual. The red machine stayed silent and motionless. It made occasional little crackling noises. The beavers followed the progress of the men for most of the afternoon. Yard by yard, they retreated in front of the humans, who were themselves advancing with great care into the forest. They seemed to be following a line along the high ridge but they kept going off for a little distance on either side. What it was they were doing mystified the beavers.

Sometime later that afternoon, Josh and Ranger returned. They had been fishing down near Port Henry for pickerel but had caught nothing. The beavers heard the sound of the engine from way off. The crows, who were also keeping a curious eye on what the men were doing, began to speculate on what would happen when Josh came ashore.

It was Ranger who noticed the helicopter first. He barked. 'What is it?' Josh called. Ranger went on barking. Josh couldn't see what it was that had attracted the dog's attention. It didn't matter a row of beans in any case. It would sink into total insignificance beside the news he had been given of the planned development. He shouted at the dog to be quiet in a voice that sounded so miserable Ranger obeyed out of sympathy for his friend.

It was not until they were on the approach run towards the landing stage that Josh saw the helicopter. The throttle died under his hand. He stiffened in disbelief and pointed. Ranger started to bark, exasperated it had taken Josh so long to see the intruders. Josh took in the tent and the group of men coming through the trees towards the shore. The anger that had been building inside him since yesterday when he had left the store surged up. His eyes became very hot and his body shook. He bent over the engine and next minute they were racing towards the beach. Ten yards out he cut the motor and jumped into knee-deep water. The boat grounded beside him as he struggled to force his way to the land. Ranger was already ashore.

The cottage door swung open and there coming to meet him was a big, beefy man smoking a cigar. A jay took off screaming its shrill warning. Josh felt pains in his chest as he ran towards the cottage. 'Hi!' The man called. 'Nice little place you got here.' Ranger never took his eyes off the stranger. He knew that this man was the threat that Josh feared. This man had dared to invade their home. He meant harm to them both. Ranger could smell it in the air all around. It was a frightening smell. Ranger went for the stranger with ears flat against his head. He leapt for the man's face.

A heavy boot caught him in the ribs. For Ranger it was the worst moment of his life. He rolled over and over, aware only of the searing pain. His mouth opened wide as he fought for air. Lights were exploding inside his head. Every bone in his body felt as if it was dissolving.

Josh almost fell over getting to him. He was in distress himself. He knelt beside the dog and cradled his head in his hands. He soothed Ranger as best he could and ran an expert hand under the dog. He buried his face in the dog's fur.

'Looks like some folks need to keep better control of their pets.' The big stranger stood beside them. From the corner of his eye, Josh could see the man's brown workboots with their reinforced steel toe plate. 'One of these days that young pup's going to be hurt, real bad!'

Josh squared up to Bourassa. His fist caught the man high up on the shoulder. Bourassa laughed and gave him a gentle slap on the face. Josh put his head down and charged. It was like running into a wall. He felt himself being crushed in a bear hug. His feet left the ground as the man lifted him and the pressure increased. An iron band was crushing his ribs. He felt the stranger laugh and the next thing he knew he was lying on the ground close to Ranger.

Bourassa shook his head at both of them and re-lit his cigar. Ranger attempted a growl but broke off with a whimper. Bourassa dropped the match on Josh's chest. 'Now see here, old man. You've got to start showing some respect round here.' He extended an arm and yanked Josh to his feet. The old man stumbled and one of the other strangers put an arm behind his shoulders to support him. Josh pushed him away, dropped to his knees and was sick.

Bourassa stood over him until he had finished. 'My company could sue you for assault for hitting me,' he announced. 'Not to mention your puppy dog friend here. Then there's a little matter of trespass. I'd say you'd be inside for six months. What do you think, guys?' The men around shuffled and looked uncomfortable.

Josh stared at the ground in humiliation. Had the world gone mad? Was this some sort of a bad dream? But the pain in his chest and Ranger's whimpers were all too real.

'What do you mean, trespass?' he muttered.

'Can't understand a word you say, old fellow,' Bourassa said. 'Speak up! A man can't have meaningful dialogue if the other party don't make sense.' He laughed.

'Who are you?' Josh asked in a more controlled voice. He wiped his mouth on the sleeve of his shirt.

'Now that's better.' The big man sketched a bow. 'Bourassa's the name. Big Brian is how folks know me. But, in your case, your special case, you can call me "Sir"!'

Josh looked at him and thought his was the face of the greedy, aggressive humanity that was going to destroy everything he believed in.

'You must be Gilpin. Joshua Gilpin. Our illegal squatter, I'll bet.'

'Illegal? What do you mean, illegal?' Josh said with more conviction than he felt. 'I've lived here for twelve years. My great grandfather built that cottage!'

'So he should have got a better lawyer,' Bourassa sneered. His voice became more menacing. 'See here old man. I'm giving you twenty eight days to quit. The president of my company reckons that's fair notice. If you're still hanging about after that, well, our 'dozers will be busy round here by then. It'll be real sad if there's an accident. That kind of thing sure slows up the work schedule.'

'Who are you people?' Josh whispered.

Bourassa grinned and flicked the ash from his cigar with deliberate exaggeration. 'We're the new owners of this piece of fly-blown real estate, that's who,' he said. 'Parker Properties Incorporated. And I'm the construction manager. Let me be the first to give you the good news, Mister Gilpin. Over the next two months, we're going to turn this dump into the biggest pleasure park east of the Rockies.' He paused to let the words sink in. Almost gently he added, 'And your cottage just happens to be right in the middle of the action. So get packing ... Now!'

He motioned the others to leave Josh where he was. He had a brief conversation with the senior surveyor and told him he'd be back the next day. Then he walked towards the helicopter. The pilot threw away a cigarette and straightened up. Bourassa gave him a nod and pointed to the rotors. The engine fired, the blades began to swing and soon the lake was filled with the familiar slap-slap noise.

On the way back to Port Henry, Bourassa became quite chatty.

'Not bad, Ed. Not a bad day's work at all. Now, a hot bath, a big juicy steak and the best room in the house will see me just fine.'

'Sounds good to me, Mr Bourassa,' said the pilot, looking straight ahead.

Back on the ground, one of the surveyors offered to help Josh get Ranger back to the cottage. The dog could walk but was in a lot of pain. He wouldn't even let Josh examine him. 'I know how you feel, old chap,' had been Josh's comment. 'You get a good night's sleep and we'll take you to the vet first thing tomorrow.'

The surveyor started to apologise for what had happened. Josh heard him out, willing him to leave so he could lick his wounds in private. 'I'll just give you one piece of advice, son,' he called after him. 'Pitch defiles everyone who touches it.'

Chipwe and Petwa eased themselves from the hiding place they had found in the bracken overlooking the cottage. They swam back to the lodge in silence. They had seen everything that had happened and while not in the least clear who the newcomers were or what they wanted, they were distressed by the attacks on Ranger and Josh. They didn't refer to it in any way later while feeding with the others but they fell asleep strangely subdued.

CHAPTER FOUR

News of the helicopter landing and the attack on Ranger soon became common knowledge to all the lake animals for miles around. The crows had seen everything. As they scavenged a couple of mornings later amongst the rubbish the surveyors had left behind, they discussed what it all meant. Opinion was divided. The humans who had appeared from the air were generous in the scraps they had left. On the other hand, the dog was injured. Josh had carried him down to the boat just after dawn the next day and had then set off across the lake. Humans usually meant trouble of some sort or other, they agreed, from the top of their favourite tree.

So the news spread far and wide. Among the lake dwellers everyone gave a sigh of relief the men had not stayed long. The noise, power and size of the red helicopter had terrified most of them. Nathan was unconvinced by their abrupt departure. 'They'll be back, you mark my words,' he warned.

Later that day, he had turned suddenly on Chipwe, who was imitating the noise the helicopter had made, and hissed in rage, 'You stop that! Don't you know it was men who killed your father.' He tried to cuff him but Chipwe was too quick and scampered into the sleeping chamber. 'I'm sorry,' Nathan said to Mataama, who had begun to bristle at him. 'I'm not feeling too good. I think I'll go outside for a while.'

In the thick forests surrounding the lake, only the black bears and the raccoons were undeterred by what had happened. Ranger was no friend of theirs. No matter how quietly they approached the cottage, Ranger always heard them and barked and barked till Josh appeared stick in hand, holding up a lamp in the other. To date, no bear or raccoon had ever been able to go through the rubbish. Indeed, it had become a point of honour among the young raccoons to be the first to do so. The prospect of more humans meant richer pickings, just so long as the animals were careful to keep out of gun range.

Brunner also heard about the red helicopter. He was going uphill across a rocky neck of land that separated two small lakes, when a grey timber wolf came out of a clump of birch trees, upwind. For a long moment, both animals stared at one another. Beavers move slowly on land and are further handicapped by poor eyesight. Brunner was no coward. Despite the recent hard winter he was still big for a beaver, weighing close to forty pounds. He scowled at the wolf and shook his large, blunt head at it. He snarled to show the size and strength of his teeth. In the end, the wolf grinned, sat down across the path and began to groom itself. After a moment or so it asked, 'And where are you heading for, my plump young beaver?'

Brunner told him.

'Well, I'd tread carefully, if I was you,' said the wolf and proceeded to tell him about the men, the red helicopter and the dog. 'Two broken ribs, I heard,' the wolf confided. 'Don't like the sound of that. Humans usually go stupid over dogs, over-feeding them and making a fuss of them. This lot strike me as being quite a different sort. I'd watch out. Nothing like a thick beaver pelt for keeping out the cold, or so I'm told!' And with that, he loped away to investigate a fresh rabbit scent.

What the wolf had said alarmed Brunner. It also reminded him that timber wolves frequently hunted in packs of up to twelve. He had been lucky, again. He shivered and trudged on for a further half mile towards the next lake. The undergrowth was low and springy and whipped at his head as he pushed through.

Later, he realised the meeting with the wolf had upset him more than he cared to admit. He wondered if he too would always be an outsider with only himself for company. He gave a little growl in the back of his throat. Animals are not sentimental by nature but they do yearn for their natural way of life.

The death of his parents and, he had to assume, of his siblings as well, had shocked Brunner to his core. At first, he had fled from the memory of a knife flashing in the sun and of a drowned mother. But there was more to it than just that. There was this compulsion to keep travelling. He was being driven by an urge to move on rather like the one migrating birds or butterflies experience. And he was only just beginning to realise what he was after.

Brunner wanted to be with his own kind. He was seeking a fresh start with beavers who would accept him and give him the companionship he craved. He wanted to be able to ignore the constant memory of the past. He wanted to belong to a proper lodge again. He wanted a mate. Otherwise he could only expect to end up as a piece of carrion for scavengers to chew and pick over.

Clouds of mosquitoes danced in front of his eyes. They were hungry and aggressive, swarming in their hundreds around his nostrils and eyelids. Almost blinded, he splashed into the shallows and sank with infinite relief into the cool waters of yet another lake.

It was the starlings who told Brunner about Nathan's lodge and the beavers living there. They had swooped down into the branches of a nearby bush, curious to meet this new arrival. They jostled one another for a perch, scolding and snapping in their excitement. If you ever want to keep a secret, never tell it to the starlings. They are incapable of using discretion. But they are good sorts for all that, always ready for a joke as they go about their business as nature's couriers.

This was how Brunner first heard about the old beaver, the twins and Mataama. The starlings also told him that the swamp above the higher dam was flooded and that the level had risen almost to the top of the dam wall. Nathan and the others were constantly out making repairs.

The birds left Brunner and flew off chattering and were soon swallowed up in the early morning mist. Later, the mist turned to rain which helped keep the mosquitoes down a little bit. Still later, the wind began to pick up strength and blow in great gusts.

The going was not easy. Brunner began to descend a steep scree, slipping as he did so on the loose, wet stones. He picked up the strong scent of a red fox and that made him hurry down all the more. It must have had its lair close by, judging by the rankness of the smell.

The wind was blustering now, driving the rain before it in stinging waves. It was one of those sudden storms that are born deep in the heart of the mountains, when two or more giant swirls of air collide, hurl thunder at each other and then decide to go off on a rampage. All round him, the fir trees braced their roots as the wind beat them almost double.

But Brunner hardly cared. He was remembering the starlings' directions and all his attention was focused on that. Besides, below the surface of the water, he was no longer affected. He swam steadily on with just the occasional lake trout for company. The fish moved their gills in studied unconcern at the muffled roar overhead.

They followed him with watchful eyes until he had swam out of their territory and their memory.

Eventually, Brunner felt the push of the river flowing all round him in a firm, rocking motion. It lifted him up for a moment and tried to turn him over on his side. Then it dropped away into the depths of the lake and the turbulence died with it. He felt elated. He knew he was getting close to the colony.

He swam harder and after a few minutes, began to hear the unmistakable sounds of a dam in trouble. They grew louder as he approached. There were creaks and wheezes and odd cracks and bangs. Brunner surfaced and drew a much needed breath. He peered around but couldn't see much in the rain. His concern grew. If the lower dam was under this sort of strain, then the top dam had to be in very real danger of collapse.

He swam ashore. It was not easy climbing up the steep bank. His hind feet scrabbled in the sodden earth and twice he almost fell back down on to the pebbles beneath. He was panting hard by the time he pulled himself over the edge and stopped for a moment to get his breath.

He had to hold his head to one side against the wind and rain, unable to face into it. Then he went as fast as he could, slipping every now and then in his haste. He could just make out the domed shape of Nathan's lodge thirty yards or so away, right up against the far bank of the river. A few moments later, he was looking down at the top dam itself.

It was a massive structure. It spanned the river like some great, bristling hedgerow, two yards high and almost as thick. A pair of beavers can build a dam in a week, but Brunner knew that this was the work of generations of animals. He also knew it couldn't last for very much longer.

The wind was piling the waters into small waves that swept on fiercely, breaking over the top of the dam. Every few seconds, the surface of the river was torn apart as the wind exploded in fierce squalls. It was almost as if the weather had singled out the dam to vent its special rage on.

Even as he watched, the middle of the dam began to bulge. Slowly at first; an infinitesimal movement. But Brunner could feel the energy building there. He saw the altered shape and, in a split second, could gauge how the profile of the wall was changing. Streams of water were starting to show. A faint shiver came from deep within the dam. And another. Now some of the small branches were splintering.

From the corner of his eye, he spotted heads break the surface close to the lodge. Four of them. He sprang up on his hind legs hissing in alarm, trying to warn them. He ran up and down in short, desperate rushes to catch their attention. From his vantage point well above them, he heard a great crack and spun round to see the centre of the dam collapse inwards and be swept away in a torrent of water that went rearing and tumbling through the breach.

It took just three seconds to reach the lodge, which it shouldered aside, and, still accelerating, to punch through the lower dam and race on towards the lake, dragging with it the tangled confusion of two dams. Of the beavers there was no trace.

In the Eagle Tavern, the air was thick with tobacco smoke. Outside, the rain splattered on the windows but here inside, it was warm and fuggy. At the best table beside an old fashioned wood stove, a waiter passed round another order of beer and rum chasers. Strong hands grasped the glasses and another loud toast was drunk.

The noise level rose. At the half dozen or so other tables along the wide mahogany bar that ran the length of the saloon, the local men listened to the loud conversation.

Port Henry had not seen men like these newcomers since the railway spur had been completed years earlier. But they had no difficulty recognising the type. Burly men with hard, battered fists who represented powerful interests, money and change ... big change.

Big Brian Bourassa, with the experience of a dozen similar situations under his belt, was enjoying himself. He lit a cheroot and exhaled a cloud of pungent blue smoke. He tipped back his chair and carefully examined the waiting, watching locals.

'Hey waiter!' he suddenly shouted. 'Give all these fine, Port Henry gentlemen here a drink of their own fancy. So come on! Fill 'em up!'

There was a whoop of approval from the crowd and a general rush to the bar.

'So when do we get started, Brian?' Luke Lopez, the number two man, asked.

'The bulldozers, the graders, the dumptrucks and support vehicles will be arriving by rail in four days. They'll be in by dusk,' Bourassa explained. 'The boss agrees with me that the sooner we start, the better.' He looked at his section heads. 'You all know what you've got to do.' He jerked a thumb towards the bar. 'Get the labour signed up. Organise the fuel and food supplies. I'm going to take a look at the old track from the station to the lake. I want to be out there working within twelve hours of the vehicles arriving. Got that?'

The others gave a shout of approval and the process of destroying Lake Napachokee got underway in earnest.

Brunner had never felt so helpless. He ran backwards and forwards along the river bank, frantically searching the waters below for any sign of the beavers. He was oblivious to the storm; his whole attention was centred on the flood of water that raced away below him. He chattered in despair as he scanned the surface for any signs of life.

It was strewn with debris and chocolate brown in colour. It was choked with branches and rocks all of which the torrent sent spinning round with skull cracking force.

Seeing this, Brunner ran back towards the lake. Here a long plume of froth and mud stretched towards the far shore until it became lost in the murk and the waves. He noted the swirl of fast moving eddies and, further out, where the whirlpools were forming at the place the river plunged down into the depths of the lake.

He reasoned that if the beavers had managed to escape the battering of the tidal wave, they would have dived deep and come up as far out in the lake as possible. They would eventually come ashore much further down from where he was standing now.

For the next couple of hours, until the rain stopped and a cold watery moon appeared over the treetops, Brunner searched. He kept to the shallows and patches of sand at the water's edge. Sometimes, he slipped on weed-covered boulders and stubbed the front of his paws. Occasionally, he had to scramble awkwardly over a tree brought down by the storm.

Every few minutes, he would pause to sit upright and whistle. It was a long, urgent call which carried far on the damp night air. Other animals heard it too and sensed its meaning. A mile away, a bob-cat stopped sharpening its claws on a spruce tree to listen. It moved its head from side to side to gauge the direction. Fierce, yellow eyes blazed in anticipation. It drew back its lips in a silent snarl, unmasking powerful incisors, and padded quickly towards the lakeshore.

Brunner was on the point of turning back when an answering whistle eventually came. A moment later he would have missed it. He had stopped on a bank of small pebbles that skittered and rattled at the slightest movement, drowning out everything else. As it was, he was not even sure he had heard it. He whistled again and then sat motionless, straining to hear.

It came again. There was no doubt this time. It gave him the information he needed. He began to run, trying to get clear of the shingles which seemed determined to pull him back. He was going inland towards the dark mass of the forest. He whistled again and the reply was closer. That was how he came to find Petwa, lying half-drowned under a rock.

The young beaver was in poor shape and half-stunned. Brunner licked his face energetically until the yearling protested. There was a great deal of soreness on one side of the youngster's head where a branch must have hit him.

At Brunner's urging they headed back towards the lake but it soon became obvious that Petwa was in distress. In the end, he clambered up on Brunner's back and clung there 'baby fashion' while Brunner began the long, slow swim back to the river. In the calm that invariably follows a storm, Brunner found the other beavers huddled together on the far bank, examining the wreck of their dams and lodge.

As Brunner approached, Petwa set up a chorus of mewings. He slid off Brunner's back and swam to meet his family. The watching beavers pressed themselves to the ground and hissed in warning and in fright. The river, swollen with the water from the swamp, still ran strongly though with nothing like its previous force. It

was too strong for Petwa and Brunner had to seize him
by the neck and carry him to the other bank, where he
let him go.

He backed off then and lay in the water swimming hard
against the current while the other beavers assessed him.
They hissed at him, frightened by the sudden appearance of this large male newcomer. Nathan bristled and
challenged him in a series of deep guttural growls. It
was all too apparent, however, that the old beaver was
in no physical condition to match his threats with action.
Mataama seized Petwa by the scruff of the neck and
dragged him away to one side where she began to groom
him, ignoring the others. Brunner remained where he
was. He knew that this was the critical moment.

Instinct told him that this meeting was all-important.
Saving a beaver from possible death in the strange-
ness of the forest was not sufficient reason for a well-
established beaver family to accept a stranger into its
ranks.

He was worse than a stranger. He was a renegade,
an outcast even. Why else would he be on his own like
this? Far from his own lodge and kin? He was a threat.
A challenger to Nathan's position as head of the family.
There could be no doubt of that. He was a threat even
to the yearlings' future dominance.

Nathan and Chipwe took to the water and circled
Brunner. Several times they shied away from him in
sudden alarm and bared their teeth in menace.

Brunner told them about himself and how the trappers
had killed his own family. He told them about the lynx
and the wolf. He described how the dam had burst and
how he'd tried to warn them. Then Petwa gave his
account of what had happened and how Brunner had
helped.

Meekly Brunner paddled ashore taking care to avoid

approaching Mataama. He began to groom himself, aware of the others watching him. His pelt was thin and in places staring. The fat in his tail was almost finished. He looked gaunt. There was nothing he could do about that. He felt his eyes closing and shook himself to stay awake. Try as he might, he could do nothing to prevent himself from falling asleep even in these life or death moments.

With one last effort he padded along the bank closest to the remains of the lodge and sank down, facing the way a predator would come. It was the last gesture he had left to make. As he fell asleep, he was dimly aware that the others had stopped hissing. Brunner hoped that this meant something.

CHAPTER FIVE

Port Henry was proud of its weekly newspaper. It gave the little place a certain style. It was not, it has to be said, the best known journal in the world and to date the only international event it had ever covered in the ninety nine years of its existence, was the 'World Frog Derby' in Orlando, Florida some three years back. And that was only because the then editor used it as an excuse for a family holiday on official expenses. He was sacked shortly afterwards by the irate publisher and owner (Theodore P. Boggs).

By now, of course, the Port Henry Times Clarion had acquired a new editor. He was a young, fresh faced, friendly man who had spent enough time in that same big city as a law student, to realise how lucky he was to be able to come up here and write a little, fish a little and converse with all and sundry a very great deal. His name was Jack Neary. Irish, some said, with a shock of curly hair.

So when he heard about Ranger being kicked in the ribs by some recently arrived red neck construction boss, his hackles went up. 'Tell me that one again, Miss Dent,' he requested.

Miss Dent had worked at the Times Clarion, woman and girl, for the last thirty two years. There was nothing she didn't know about running a newspaper. She was blessed with an amazing memory and enjoyed her own prominent position in local society to the full.

'Well, Mr Neary,' she said, carefully arranging her

dress as she sat down on the old hard-backed chair across the desk from her editor. 'From what I can gather from Mr Patel, our senior veterinary surgeon, Josh Gilpin, that nice, quaint old man who lives out on Lake Napachokee...' her voice continued like the grave twittering of an earnest mistle thrush. Neary listened intently. His journalistic instincts were working overtime.

Things were going better than Mataama could ever have thought possible. And it was Brunner who had made the difference, as she had known he would. Twenty four hours after the river had burst through, the water level was almost back to normal and work re-building the lower dam had begun in earnest.

At first light the beavers had studied the extent of the damage. By then, the torrent was no more than a quiet flow of water that eased itself past the boulders and the odd stake of what had once been a dam.

Brunner kept a respectful distance from them and behind Nathan, in particular. He ventured no opinion as they splashed through the deep pools left behind by the washout, assessing what needed to be done. Later, they had all swum through the swamp in single file to feed on a stand of juicy young aspens. Mataama led the way with Nathan bringing up the rear of the family. Every now and then the old beaver would turn to face Brunner and bare his teeth in warning.

For Brunner, it was a time of intense anxiety. Despite the older male's hostility he had not been totally rejected by the group. Petwa and Chipwe had both swum up to him at the start of the day before being warned off by Nathan. Mataama, while not overtly friendly, made no visible effort to drive him away.

Gratefully, Brunner swam after them but found his

own food away from the rest. For the first time in days he was able to eat as much as he wanted in safety. The others watched him as they shredded the bark between their front teeth to get at the sappy wood underneath.

Mataama studied Brunner closely. She saw the fur raised over the weals left behind by the lynx's attack and noted how he winced and kept grooming his bruised ribs. She liked the way he paused in between mouthfuls to listen and scan the area for any sign of danger. She remembered how he had brought Petwa back to her and her eyes softened.

She finished eating and licked her paws for any last dribbles of sap. Then she moved closer to Nathan. The old beaver was impatient to start work for a variety of reasons. The night had been a wretched one for him. After midnight, a sudden sharp frost had descended which froze the water in his outer coat making sleep all but impossible. He had realised in those early hours just how old he was getting and the discovery alarmed him. All the more reason to get rid of this interfering newcomer and he glared at Brunner with rising dislike.

Together with Mataama he agreed what needed to be done to repair the damage. For his part, Brunner remained in the background contenting himself helping Petwa and Chipwe stack stones and branches into neat piles for the damn builders.

After an hour it was clear that Nathan was beginning to flag. Very soon after, he got into trouble. He needed to position a particularly heavy log as a buttress but its weight and the sheer effort of lifting it vertically was too much for him. Twice he tried, but even with Mataama's efforts the log rolled back into the river. Mataama looked round in desperation, met Brunner's eye and gave a low whistle. The three of them spent the next ten minutes jockeying the branch into place.

After this, they paused and Brunner found himself deciding with them what to do next. A little later, Nathan slipped away along the riverbank to check on the flow of water entering the swamp. Brunner and Mataama started to work as a team, steadily building on what was left of the old foundations.

There was no shortage of building materials. The melting snows from the mountains had brought down whole trees and branches of all sizes, while the banks of the river were littered with wreckage from the old dams.

Together they drove thick branches vertically into the soft mud of the river bed. They plugged the gaps in-between with the stones Chipwe and Petwa carried from the rocky screes nearby. Nathan contented himself by checking to make sure the design of the new dam conformed to the flow of the river and the position of the banks at either side. They all helped thread the smaller sticks in-between the stakes, holding them between their teeth while their fingers twisted and pushed them in tightly. It was rather like weaving an enormous basket.

Hour after hour they worked, felling the young aspen trees that grew in thickets beside the swamp and gnawing them into manageable lengths. They seized the cut branches in their jaws and dragged them back through the water to the building site. Gradually, the flow of the river to the lake ceased and began to creep up the sides of the banks, deepening steadily. By the end of four days, the dam was solid and the entrance to the old lodge three feet under water.

Brunner and Nathan decided to use the same site for the new lodge and re-build it from scratch.

There was an unspoken truce now operating between the two males. Nathan no longer bared his teeth or hissed but he made it clear that there was no love

lost on his part. He hoped the stranger would go away
when the lodge was finished. He would not welcome any
change to the established order of things. He paid more
attention than usual to the young beavers as a way of
encouraging Mataama's favour.

All five of them swam and splashed their way to a particularly thick clump of trees where Brunner explained
what had to be done. To build the strongest possible
lodge he would need two different lengths of stick cut.
For the roof of the chamber, these should be a metre long.
Those that would provide the framework of the walls
around the entrance, should not be longer than half a
metre. They had to be cut as exactly as possible to this
size to allow Mataama and himself to work as efficiently
and as quickly as possible. Living out in the open for
twenty-four hours a day was not a comfortable experience for a beaver. It was too much like tempting fate.

The sticks needed to be peeled, carried back and
placed in separate heaps on the high bank above the
lodge. They set to at once, working independently and
because a beaver can gnaw through a ten centimetre
tree trunk in less than five minutes, it didn't take too
long before they were able to start building the lodge.

While the others kept the sticks coming in a steady
shuttle, Nathan and Brunner agreed on the plan to build
a spacious main chamber some four metres in diameter
and a smaller, metre-high, sleeping chamber. Extensions
would come later. So while Brunner pushed in the small
sticks to form an outline, Nathan pressed mud firmly
in-between them, using his chin and forefeet to pack it
in hard. Later, they used the longer sticks to form the
roof.

Slowly the lodge took shape. Within two days they
had fashioned both chambers and were thinking of
excavating a further room inside the bank itself. But

because the sun was so strong, they added layer upon layer of branches which they packed with mud and stones until it set hard, like concrete. Seven days after the beavers had been washed out, Nathan, Mataama, the twins and now Brunner slept under a new roof. As Chipwe said when it was finished, did anyone mind if he went straight to sleep?

Petwa and Chipwe were scouting the men. An hour or so earlier, the red helicopter had flown up the lake from the direction of Port Henry and had once again landed in a storm of wind, dust and howling noise. They had dived deep and swam back to the lodge.

'It's trouble,' was Nathan's only comment.

'Why don't we go back and keep an eye on what the humans are doing?' Petwa suggested.

'Then we'll know what they're up to,' added Chipwe.

'All right,' said Mataama. 'But be careful. This is not a game any more. Nathan's right. This could be bad news for us all.'

After they had gone, she thought for a long while. Eventually she said, 'I think I'll go and take a look at the old burrow in the bank and see what condition it's in. You never know if we might need it,' she added looking at Brunner.

So while Nathan and Brunner went on excavating another chamber deep inside the earth bank, she swam with the lake current for a long time to the hide Nathan had made many years ago as a refuge from the fur trappers. Chipwe and Petwa, in the meantime, eased their way across the swamp and into the forest, to see what the men were up to.

On clear, sunny days in the North, sound carries easily. There is usually a playful breeze to see that it does. On this particular day, the air was also full of the promise of the summer to come: the scent of resin from the pine trees, the yeasty spray of sap, the smell of sunlight on green leaves and bursting flower buds. In the forest clearings, butterflies danced and swooped and sang with the sheer delight of being alive. Along the edges of the swamp, brilliant purple and red dragonflies were hunting mosquitoes.

Chipwe and Petwa had no problem locating where the strange men had got to. This was very easy because the birds were giving continuous commentary on their movements. The helicopter had been parked on top of what had been Josh's vegetable patch. They had put on large bundles and started trekking into the bush towards the far side of the river where a rutted and damaged track led overland to Port Henry.

All the lakeshore animals were intensely curious to discover why the men had come back and what they were doing. They were also waiting to see what would happen when the blackfly found them. Blackfly are amongst the worst biting insects known to Nature. In human terms they are tiny, barely the size of a large pin head. Yet their bite will draw blood and frequently does. They have the dreadful ability to get inside anything and everything, like so many grains of sand. All animals are painfully aware of them and the danger they pose.

It is not only humans who have been driven mad after hours of their silent, biting torture. Great elks and moose alike have been found roaring in pain and dashing their heads against tree trunks in helpless agony. In the early summer in the North, at the time when Bourassa and his party were pushing their way through waist-high clumps of springy elder saplings and stumbling over tussocks of rough marsh grass, blackfly are king. They should be avoided at all costs.

*　　*　　*

The men's voices grew hoarse from shouting. Tempers frayed as the hot morning sun glared down, the sweat starting to run into their eyes. There was no let up, no escape from the millions of hungry, biting, fanatical flies that massed round their heads looking for all the world like so many thick black veils. But Bourassa's team was tough. They might curse and complain and even bellow at times but doggedly they laid out yard after yard of white marker tape. They wound it round trees and in and out of the bigger saplings; in marshy areas, they drove tall stakes into the ground and stapled the tape to the top of the posts. By the time they reached the river and flung themselves face down into the water, a curious path stretched far behind them into the distance.

'It's like some sort of channel,' thought Chipwe.

'They've gone mad,' Petwa said with satisfaction. 'The flies have got 'em.'

'No,' said Chipwe, thinking hard. 'I don't reckon so. Remember, they carried that white bark or whatever it is, out here with them. So they must have a reason for doing it. It's deliberate.'

'Well, you tell me what it's for,' Petwa challenged. 'I mean, you can't swim along it, can you!'

Chipwe thought long and hard. By this time, the blackfly had found them too and were beginning to crowd round, going for their eyelids and ears.

'I've got it!' he cried all of a sudden, making Petwa jump. 'Don't you see?' He tugged at his brother's ear. 'It's just like us using pieces of birch bark to mark a trail and show others, like Mataama and Nathan, where to come later.'

Petwa spat the piece of twig he had been chewing out of his mouth. 'If that's so,' he said in a quiet, unemotional tone, 'then can I ask if you have any ideas who – or what – might be coming? And when?'

*   *   *

The burrow was still there. Mataama had problems finding the entrance. It was silted over and she had to dig and scrape away the debris that blocked it. Once inside though, she found the main living chamber intact though cold and uninviting. The roof had collapsed in one place and a pile of earth took up most of one corner. It would need shoring up for certain. But it existed and no other animal seemed to have used it. It was roomy and it could be made habitable. The storerooms opening off were also serviceable, though quite empty. She spent a busy hour deciding what needed to be done just in case these men interfered in all their lives.

The crows in the fir tree were unsettled. A strong evening breeze had sprung up, the result of changing arctic air systems many miles overhead. Up in the stratosphere, wind flows were gaining strength. On Lake Napachokee, the crows had to tighten their grip on branches, an unconscious gesture but one that was irritating none-theless. To fall off one's perch is not too cool a thing to have happen to you. Not if you're a bird, that is.

Inevitably, a slanging match developed and they began to scold one another. During the winter months crows, like all birds, are too busy surviving, trying to eat their own body weight each day, keeping warm and avoiding eagles or the bigger buzzards, to have much time to worry about anything else. But a crow's sub-conscious mind misses nothing. Everything it sees is noted and stored away so that by the following May, there exists in each and every crow, a positive encyclo-pedia of hearsay, supposition or good old-fashioned gossip just clamouring to be aired.

This evening was no exception. Young birds, admitted a few weeks ago into the sophistication of adult crow life, sat statue-like, their beaks open in amazement. Among their more experienced elders outrage upon outrage built up in frenzied shrieks until the accusations collapsed in a welter of caw-cawing or laughter. Until someone else began it all over again, and there was never any shortage of innuendo.

'Wake up Brunner! Wake up!' Petwa was shaking his shoulder. 'Brunner! Oh please wake up will you! There's something happening outside.'

They swam out and clambered on top of the lodge where it was very dark indeed. As his eyes got used to the blackness, Brunner saw there were no stars. It was overcast and there was a smell of the rain in the air that would be here by tomorrow.

'What is it?' he demanded. He felt tetchy. He had, after all, been sound asleep.

'Listen!' said Chipwe. The wind pushed through the tops of the trees. A couple of them creaked in protest.

'There it is again,' Chipwe was insistent. 'Can't you hear it? There! I promise you it isn't my imagination.'

The others joined them and they all stood in the open perfectly still, straining their ears. Concentrating ... but on what? Brunner wondered. And then he heard a sound like a snatch of far distant thunder. It faded and he had almost dismissed it from his mind when it came again, if anything louder. Petwa had heard it too. The beavers waited listening for it. They were puzzled.

As it grew louder, Brunner realised it wasn't like any thunder he had ever heard before. Whereas thunder has a majestic echoing roll across the heavens this sound, whatever it was, was somehow intermittent. Loud but jerky. There was something else about it. Something uncomfortable. It was an aggressive, greedy sort of noise, not unlike the sound of the outboard engine in Josh's boat, only a thousand times deeper. Brunner realised with a shock that it was beginning to make his fur bristle. There was a definite sensation of menace, deep in the heart of the roar.

'What's that light? There! And look! There!' Petwa demanded, pointing into the night. Strange things were happening in the sky. Brief explosions of yellow came and went, fingering the clouds overhead as if a giant will-o'-the-wisp was struggling to fly. Then the growling, grating sound disappeared almost as if it had sunk into the earth.

A silence fell and there was a sensation of Nature itself holding its breath, waiting and watching with a mounting sense of apprehension. No night birds called. There was no barking from Ranger. Even the frogs in the swamp were silent. The minutes passed agonisingly slowly at first, then more quickly as a little flicker of relief began to be felt. Perhaps it was nothing at all to have got so concerned about. Some trick of the weather, perhaps?

Then closer, much closer, the Beast jumped out of the blackness! For a terrible moment they stared at a writhing snake-like monster with great glaring eyes that illuminated everything in front of it. An angry snarling creature that spat yellow fire and lurched towards them. On the night breeze came a smell they had never met before. A horrible smell. A smoky, burning, choking smell. It was the breath of the monster itself!

The beavers dived headlong into the river. Terror seized Brunner. He began to swim in circles, panic freezing his limbs. The others came to the surface, breathless with fright.

'Brunner! Petwa!' Chipwe spluttered. 'The markers! The white markers! We've got to hide them.' He spluttered in the effort to tread water. 'Don't you see! The

Monster's following them! Quick! It'll find us here in the river if we don't destroy the markers. Come on!'

They scrambled up the steep bank, paws scraping for purchase on tree roots and stones. Petwa and Chipwe scampered ahead, threading a path through the undergrowth, splashing across the swamp, no effort made at any form of concealment. Their hearts pounded, the blood hammered in their heads. On and on and on. Racing, because their lives depended on it. Nathan's head was flung back as he tried to keep up with them. They began to string out. Their mouths were open, their breath coming in painful, whoop-like gasps.

And then ahead of them, gleaming very faintly in the darkness, were the white lines the monster needed. Each beaver caught the marker, gnawed it in ferocious concentration and chewed it through in eight places before they realised it still stretched far away on either side. They couldn't destroy it. It was far too long. There was no way they could alter the pathway.

Beneath them, the ground began to shiver. It started to shake. They could feel the vibrations running through their paws. Every hair on Chipwe's body lifted on end. A huge blinding eye caught him in the middle of the track. He stood there. Transfixed. Paws frozen to his sides as the bucking, crashing thing ran straight at him. Its breath was all round him. A gust of hot, oily air engulfed him. There was noise everywhere. He was living in a nightmare. With a shriek, the Monster leapt at him! He felt himself falling...

CHAPTER SIX

'Hello old chap. You must be Ranger.' Jack Neary stood by the front porch of Josh's cottage. He made encouraging noises to the dog standing above him. It was a delightful day and Jack was feeling in the best of moods. Ranger gave a few more barks but it was clear from the way he wagged his tail that he had taken an instant liking to this new human.

'And who might you be?' came a voice from inside the small cottage. Neary told him. After a pause the old man came out, blinking in the bright sunlight. In his right hand he carried a heavy stick. 'Can't be too careful these days,' he said, watching the editor's face, and invited Jack in.

Neary took the proffered chair while Ranger, after a few half-hearted growls, came over and gave him a thorough sniffing. Before long he let Jack fondle his ears.

'You're the first man in a long while he's let do that,' Josh commented.

'I was very sorry to hear about Ranger's ... accident,' Jack replied, chucking him under the chin. The old man snorted.

'Accident! That was no accident, Mister. Just downright wickedness.' He picked up the stick beside him and pointed it in the direction of the construction camp. Several portacabins could be seen on top of the rise, overlooking the lakeshore. Smoke was coming from a metal stove pipe chimney. Someone was playing a radio.

'You being an editor, a man of the world and all that, you'll know about these people.'

Neary gave a nod. 'Big company, Mr Gilpin. Lots of friends in high places.'

'And they hire a real low life to flatten any opposition,' Josh interrupted with real bitterness. He wiped a damp sleeve across his brow then looked at Jack. 'Heck!' he apologised. 'I'm forgetting all the manners my old mother ever taught me. You've come quite a way, Mr Neary. It's thirsty work heading up the lake. How about a cup of coffee? 'Fraid I can't get you anything stronger.'

Later, after Josh had poured them both a cup of bitter-tasting coffee from an enamel jug that stood on top of the old iron range, Neary asked, 'I heard you were told to get out.'

'Something like that,' Josh nodded.

'So the question I'm asking is how come you're still here?'

The old man chuckled and reached in his pocket for a box of matches. He took his time lighting the pipe, holding the matchbox across the top of the bowl for a faster burn. 'Why don't you ask Mister Bourassa that? Seems like it's his lake these days.'

'Maybe I will,' Neary replied. 'But I'd like to know from you first. Off the record, if you know what I mean.'

The old man considered. He puffed on his pipe a few times with evident enjoyment. He looked down at the dog and patted him.

'What do you think, Ranger? Should we trust him?' The dog wagged its tail.

'If you want the truth,' said Josh after a further pause, 'I'm not in their way right now. I stay indoors. Guess I have to, in case someone took it into their head to have a look round and help themselves to whatever they fancied. Besides, from what I hear, they're finding it a whole lot tougher going than they thought.' He indicated the surrounding trees.

'See those redwoods? They were ancient when my great grand-daddy first settled here way back in 1895. Why, they've got roots that must go down to Australia, by now,' he said with a chuckle. 'Guess they're like me ... old, stubborn and hard to move.'

From further down the lakeshore, a powerful engine revved up in a series of wheel spinning jerks. The acrid smell of a burning clutch soon wafted to them. 'See what I mean?' said Josh. 'I think Mister Bourassa is starting to find it's going to take a whole lot longer than he bargained for, to scrape the land bare for all those nasty little holiday homes.'

Jack looked up from the pad on his knee. Something the old man said had struck a chord in his memory. 'Did you say it was your great grandfather who settled this place back in 1895?' he asked. 'Sure did,' Josh said with pride. 'Why, he came up with the old railroad and liked it here.' He took his pipe out and gesticulated with it. 'He built this very house you're sitting in. He and a couple of Indians he trained up.'

'That's very interesting' said Jack thoughtfully. 'I was reading something about that when I was going through the archives during my first month or so in the job. There's something else about those settlements round here about that time that's important. Something to do with the land rights, as I recall. I'll have to look it up one of these days.'

Josh grunted and reached for the matchbox once again. In between puffs he said drily, 'Well, don't let your interest in history get in the way of reporting what's happening out here right now.'

They talked for a while longer and drank some more coffee. Out in the lake, a large fish jumped. Jack sighed and said it was time he took his leave. 'Pity you didn't bring a rod with you,' Josh remarked, noticing his interest. 'Best fishing in the North round here. All be in private hands in a couple of months. Think about it.'

As he shook hands, Jack felt a warm glow of admiration for the retired railwayman. He also felt a strange premonition that he had been given a clue, a vital clue to help Josh stay on in the place he loved. Jack thought this over as he trudged along the beach to where a heavy machine was at work. For the life of him though, he couldn't put his finger on quite what it was...

A few minutes later he was standing beside a gang of men watching a bulldozer filling in a huge hole. The stump and roots of a tree lay to one side. 'Tough going?' he asked a local man he recognised. The fellow nodded. His hair was black with sweat.

'You can say that again. Never known anything like it. It's strange,' he confided. 'It's as if these trees round here know what we're up to and they're refusing to die. But this'll be the last difficult one to shift.'

'How's that?' asked Neary.

The man laughed. 'Because the boss is going to dynamite the rest of them. There's a special consignment of explosives being flown in this afternoon.'

Chipwe woke up and wondered where he was. He lay quite still for a moment, letting his eyes get used to the darkness. He could hear the comforting sound of water all round him and the musky scent of beaver was everywhere. He felt warm but quite tired and his head had begun to ache. He gave a whimper and curled back up into the bark shavings, holding his front paws over his ears to try and block out the pain. It didn't seem to do much good. After a while, he got to his feet and was still complaining to himself when

Mataama's head appeared in front of him, in a swirl of water.

She pulled herself up into the lodge, wiped at her eyes, and give him a sympathetic whistle. 'How are you feeling?' she asked. And then for an awful moment it all came back to him. The glaring eye, the noise, the smell, everything! He scurried round the chamber trying to find a way out. He almost fell over her in his fright, but Mataama caught him and held him to her.

She licked him and soothed the top of his head with her paws in silent reassurance. Her confidence and calmness had its effect on him. Slowly the panic subsided and Chipwe became more settled. He sat beside the entrance and splashed water over his muzzle. Then he drank long and greedily. Afterwards, he let Mataama groom him.

'What was it?' he asked her at last. 'You must tell me. Was it a monster or a water spirit?'

Mataama made a clicking noise with her tongue and made him sit down. 'It's the men,' she said. 'It was a monster but not like any we've ever heard of. There are many of them. They all belong to the men. You'll see.' She stopped grooming him and picked up a piece of bark. Chipwe took it from her and began to nibble at it.

'Brunner pulled you out of the way,' Mataama told him. 'You must thank him. Now, I think you need more sleep so I'll leave you.'

Chipwe put his nose against hers and breathed very gently into her nostrils, which is the way beavers have of saying 'Thank you' and 'I love you'. He lay awake for a few minutes after she had slipped away but the river outside lulled him into a deep, forgetting kind of sleep.

Later, Chipwe joined the others. They were doing exactly the same as every other animal in the vicinity.

They were spying on the strange men and the vast yellow monsters that after hours of standing still, would suddenly explode into clouds of choking fumes and start their frenzied tearing up of the ground and the trees. It was not just bewildering. The beavers found the sheer scale of the destruction quite incomprehensible.

The humans themselves were just like ants, scurrying here and there, waving and gesticulating at each other. It was the yellow monsters they used to do the work for them that frightened the animals. Their strength was terrifying. They could drag out whole tree stumps with the same ease that a beaver could gnaw through a young branch. Others could claw more rock and soil out of the ground in one grab than all the beavers in the North could, even if they were to work at it for a whole month.

So absorbed were they in what the monsters were doing, that they almost failed to notice the party of men approaching their hiding place from the flank. Nathan suddenly hissed very loudly into Brunner's ear. 'Hey! Wake up! Or are you planning on making some sort of hero's last stand!' He indicated the crowd of men walking towards the bullrushes they were hiding in. A couple of strange dogs had also appeared and were bounding ahead of the men, keen to serve their human masters. Brunner followed Nathan and slid silently away into the safety of the lake. He wondered why dogs were always so untrustworthy.

From the helicopter's point of view it looked like a gigantic film set. The helicopter had flown in half an hour ago and dropped off its cargo of red-painted boxes. Now, while the men below primed the charges, Mr Sekri had decided he wanted a grandstand view of proceedings.

The pilot hovered just over the lake. Ashore, tiny

fingers scurried around the huge tree; then came a sudden flash of flame, the dull boom of an explosion, and a second later, the slow fall of a four hundred year old fir tree which bounced a couple of times, after it had hit the ground.

'Gotcha!' thought Mr Sekri in silent pleasure. Thanks to the dynamite, they'd be well up to meeting the very tight schedules he had given that ape, Bourassa. Not that he'd be telling him, of course. Far better to keep him on the usual knife edge of uncertainty. Bourassa had produced his most memorable efforts in the past when under the threat of instant dismissal. Mr Sekri saw no point in departing from a well-tried formula.

For some twelve minutes, the boss of Parker Properties Incorporated kept his helicopter busy overhead, swinging this way and that, up and down the lakeshore, while he carefully aligned his map to check on the sheer size of his newly-acquired piece of wilderness. He had already got two potential buyers for the resort. The lawyers were talking; the accountants doing their sums and his advertising agency were even now starting the creative process to help finalise the deal in a gush of superlatives.

'Make a wide arc then put me down on the far side!' he ordered. The nose of the helicopter dipped obediently. The pilot began to circle, looking ahead for the best place to land. Mr Sekri sat forward in his seat and enjoyed the sense of ownership he always felt at the start of every project. No one could see the thin smile of pleasure as he savoured the commercial possibilities beneath him. In his mind's eye he was already visualising how it would look in only a few weeks time.

He gazed out of the glass bubble ahead of him. Yes! There was that old fool's cottage. Mr Sekri noted the ragged line of washing hanging outside and the dog barking up at him. He scowled. Why was the man still hanging around? Why wouldn't he take the money and go? Oh well, Bourassa could be relied upon to sort out that problem when the time came. Mr Sekri switched his attention back to the progress that had been made.

They hadn't done too badly, he considered. Half the immediate lake shore had been denuded of trees. The earth movers had carved out the first of the flat, wide terraces needed for phase one of the development. From his vantage point, he estimated that the landscaping operation was more or less halfway to final completion.

The helicopter traversed the lake shore then began to swing back before making its landing. As it tilted, Mr Sekri caught sight of the river and with an expert's eye for detail, noted the two beaver dams stretching right across. He stared at them for a moment in total disbelief. Then, he flicked the intercom switch.

'Take me over the river,' he hissed. He stabbed a finger towards the dams. Obediently, the machine banked, hung in the air for a moment like an over-heavy pigeon, then swooped very low until the down draught from its rotors sent agitated waves slapping up against the side of the lodge. A loose branch was torn out and flung away.

Inside the cabin, Mr Sekri's face darkened. Beavers! He didn't know much about wild animals but he knew that beavers simply devoured wood. He thought of his holiday cabins and all the white-painted pine sidings that would be arriving any day now. He shivered. It was like letting a child loose in a sweet shop. Of all the animals to have right beside a brand new construction site!

He began to shake with rage. Bourassa! That fool Bourassa! What did the man think he was playing at? Here was a whole colony of dangerous animals almost on the doorstep of his prestigious development. A development built from pre-fabricated wooden house parts. It was as suicidal as letting a posse of tax inspectors loose on one's personal accounts. There was only one thing to do.

'Dynamite those beavers,' he snarled, banging his hands on his knee in impatience.

'Excuse me, sir?' the pilot asked, worried in case he had missed something.

Mr Sekri ignored him and circled the place on his map where the dams were with a thick blue pencil. When he had done this he looked across at the pilot. 'You've got sixty seconds to get back on the ground if you want to keep your job!' Mr Sekri was going to put the biggest flea there ever was in Bourassa's ear. The sooner that beaver settlement went, the better!

CHAPTER SEVEN

Nathan was sitting on top of the lodge enjoying the early summer sun. Just after dawn, a mist had risen from the lake, shrouding the tops of the pine trees and blotting them from view. For an hour, the beaver's world had become an impenetrable fog in which every sound was distorted. The sudden splash of a trout over on the far side of the lake seemed very close. Whereas the early morning honking of a flight of mallard on its way to Port Henry had echoed round for some time after the birds had gone over.

Later, the sun had burnt through and the lake began to preen itself in the warmth of this attention. The sandy bottom in the shallows grew clearer. Shadows made by overhanging fir branches darkened to form mysterious tunnels, while the deeper waters of the lake grew expansive and turned a brilliant blue.

In the reeds close to the far shore, an old rogue pike lay motionless, its jaws slightly open. This was Grancha, the most evil creature in the lake. Yesterday, she had taken two young moorhens. The placid surface of the lake had twice witnessed a sudden, great swirl as the pike came out of the depths to seize a victim in her terrible jaws, and drag it under. Grancha was over four foot long. Her skin was scarred from a hundred encounters with rivals and with man. Josh was her sworn enemy.

For years, the two of them had duelled. Grancha took special delight in taking the catch from the man's fishing line. Many times Josh had pulled out a promising bass only to find it had been neatly severed just behind the gills. Twice Josh had hooked the pike but on both occasions she had broken free. The last time, the great fish had managed to catch Josh's hand in a sideways swipe of her jaws that had cut his thumb open to the bone. There were rumours that Grancha had also taken several beaver kits in the course of her long life. Right now, her hunger was satisfied. She was content to let the current wash in and out of her mouth and wait to see what the day would bring.

Nathan rested his chin on his forepaws and day-dreamed. He tired easily these days. The clamour of the younger beavers made him irritable. It was a real delight to come up here and lie in the hot sun and listen to the gentle sounds of the water.

He had had a good life. Not that it had been remarkable in any way. He had never felt the restless urge to see other lakes or find new habitats. He had been born in this very lodge and grown up on Lake Napachokee. He had taken Jade as his mate and had brought her back here. She had died in the dreadful winter when the ice and snow had lain on the ground for close on eight months. It was a time he never wanted to see again. No winter before or since rivalled it for its killing frosts. It was a time few beavers these days could even comprehend.

The water had frozen solid right to the lodge entrance. Locked under it, Jade had given birth to their first cub Keatta, which means 'free spirit', at a time when their food supplies were almost finished. In a frenzy, Nathan attacked the ice that was keeping them imprisoned again and again. He fought the ice with all the strength at his command. He slashed at it with both teeth and claw. But it proved unrelenting and impervious to his increasing desperation. He did everything he knew to break through but it gave no sign of yielding.

Exhausted, the two grown beavers had fallen asleep cradling their baby between them, feeling the beat of its tiny heart while it suckled.

By the time the thaw finally came and they could hear the ice sheet groaning and breaking up in great splintering cracks, Jade had died of starvation. The next day, Nathan had finally burst his way up through the ice into a grey outer world. He could barely swim, so weakened was he from hunger and the cold. It had taken him a long time to scrabble a way through the slush to get at the bark of the nearest clump of willows. He had eaten and eaten, stuffing himself with the life-giving food. On his return to the lodge, he had dragged Jade's body clear then set about chewing pieces of bark into a pulp with which to feed Keatta.

But his efforts were in vain. The baby beaver would have nothing to do with the only nourishment his father could provide. Instead, he spat it out and continued to shake with hunger. In resignation, Nathan cuddled the cub with his own body and licked it and gave it all the warmth he was capable of. The brief exhilaration he had felt when he had at last succeeded in breaking through the ice mocked him now with each frantic mew the baby uttered.

Those had been terrible days. Keatta was not even weaned and refused the only food he could bring. Nathan lay there and almost gave up. His beloved Jade lay stiff and frozen close by while their cub tortured him with its cries. Heart-rending cries that went on and on until Nathan, maddened by frustration, dragged the cub by the scruff of the neck down into the water and brought it choking and coughing to the surface. To the very same place where he now lay.

And there, while the rain poured down the youngster eventually fed on a mess of waterweed Nathan had brought in what had seemed a final act of despair. Once the cub had chewed the weed and swallowed it, it had screamed for more. Later, it had been violently sick but Nathan didn't mind. He hugged Keatta, oblivious to everything. There was hope. It was going to survive.

That night, they both slept the healing oblivion nature sends animals who have reached the end of their endurance. For sixteen hours, they lay motionless until hunger awoke the cub. That day, Nathan buried Jade deep in the river bank. He filled in the entrance to the tunnel he had dug and covered the outside with stones and branches, to deter scavengers like the red fox. He shut himself away from the baby and sat hugging himself in sheer misery and loneliness. In the end, he couldn't ignore Keatta's protests any longer. The fury of the cub's cries dragged him away from his pain and he went back to the task of feeding their baby.

As the months and then the years went by, the beavers became inseparable. They foraged together; they shared responsibilities. Together, they extended the dams and enlarged the canal system above the top dam for a further fifty yards into the forest beyond. Some said it was because of his experience in looking after the infant beaver and the closeness that grew between them that Nathan never took another mate. But all the time, he grieved for Jade and at night he would sleep with a small piece of her fur, in which her scent was just present, between his paws.

It was Nathan who taught the rapidly growing cub the beauties and the dangers of Nature. He showed him animal tracks and how to recognise the scent of such predators as the lynx and the bobcat. These are solitary hunters who lie along tree branches, ready to pounce on any careless beaver dawdling along beneath. Together they escaped from a surprise pack of wolves who almost caught them in the open and who howled all night from the river bank.

One bitterly cold winter, a brown bear came to investigate the scent of beaver it had picked up along the lake shore. They had listened to it tearing at the outsides with its long, raked claws and heard it pounding and kicking, trying to break in. The strength of the lodge had defeated it and after a time, they heard it shuffle away, moaning to itself. Above all, Nathan warned his cub about men and their clever allies, the dogs.

When Keatta had become mature and had taken a mate, Nathan had accepted her warmly. He gave up the large sleeping chamber he had once shared with Jade and moved to smaller, more remote quarters elsewhere in the lodge.

Mataama had come to the lodge as a stranger to these parts. Her own family lived way down to the south of Lake Henry. Her name meant Tranquillity and her good nature and gentleness had reassured the old beaver that there would always be a place for him here. For a couple of years they had lived in total contentment within the unique social structure of a beaver family. The kits had come at regular yearly intervals: first, a sad, little stillborn and then the twins, Chipwe and Petwa.

For Nathan, they had been happy years. Then a hunting party from Port Henry had camped further down the lake. It had been their dogs who had picked up beaver scent and cornered Nathan's only cub far away from the lodge in the forest beyond the swamp. Trapped, Keatta had defied them with his sharp teeth until the sound of their barking had alerted the men, who had come at a run unslinging their rifles. They had shot him and taken his body away with them.

Nathan stirred and squeezed his eyelids together very tightly. He swallowed and blinked back the sudden pricks of memory. It would always hurt, always be there. Sometimes the past was more real to him than the everyday present. Perhaps that was why he failed to hear the men approaching sooner, on that warm summer morning that was to end so tragically.

Coming from the direction of the construction camp were more than a dozen humans armed with pickaxes, shovels and heavy wooden clubs. Two of them carried ropes and a red wooden box. Four dogs ran in amongst them, barking in excitement.

Being a Sunday, the men were entitled to start work an hour later than usual and Bourassa's suggestion of a 'little bit of sport before breakfast' had been a popular one. Bourassa had originally intended to use one of the great earth moving machines to clear both dams and the lodge out of the way. But a closer inspection the evening before however had shown it to be impossible.

The men had reached the point on the bank where the upper dam stretched across the river. From here, they began to pick their way along the top of it in single file. They made careful progress as their combined weight made the dam sway and even rock at times. Cursing as they stumbled, they made their way along it. Below them, the dogs alternately swam or splashed their way through deep pools or across rocky shallows. They sensed even more adventure to come.

Nathan lifted his head and looked around. His nostrils quivered as he sniffed at the morning. There was no sign of Chipwe or Petwa or even this newcomer, Brunner. They were supposed to be working on the lower dam downstream but he couldn't see them anywhere.

Then, in an instant, Nathan was wide awake. He sat up on his haunches, every instinct alert. He couldn't see anything yet but he could hear men and dogs coming this way.

The skin round his muzzle crawled with fright. He bared his teeth and snarled. His fur bristled. He snuffed at the air but there was no mistake. The men were getting nearer. Their scent was stronger. Now he could hear their shouts and the noise their boots made. He could hear laughter and the commands they gave their dogs.

He whistled a warning to the others as loud as he could. He did so again and yet again but there was no response from any of the younger beavers. Nathan was in a quandary. Did he have sufficient time to swim and warn them? What about Mataama down below in the lodge? It was while he was trying to decide what to do first that he saw the dog.

It had scrambled up on top of the bank, its coat dripping with water. It shook itself with a powerful shrug. It was a rangy looking brute with the look of wolf about its head and shoulders. It looked around then came on. It was not far ahead of the men whose shouts by now could be clearly heard.

Nathan dived. There was no point waiting any longer. His fear was such that his strength seemed to be deserting him, just when he needed it most. The power in his tail and webbed hind feet was not there any more. He forced himself down under the water, fighting the panic that rose in his throat. Gasping for breath, he swam awkwardly to the entrance at the very bottom of the lodge. Somewhere above he could hear Mataama singing.

Petwa yawned and rubbed a muddy paw over his brow. He looked round him at the work they had completed that morning. They had done well. They had packed yet another layer of mud and stones into the dam wall in anticipation of the storms to come next winter, and already it was setting hard. He felt hungry and decided it was time to go and find something to eat.

He climbed up to the top of the dam and stopped for a moment to bask in the sunshine. For a while he sat there blinking while his eyes got used to the glare off the water. He looked upstream towards the lodge and noticed that Nathan had gone back inside. He could hear Chipwe and Brunner clambering up to join him and he was on the point of turning to greet them when he saw something that made his blood run cold.

Making their way along the upper dam was a party of men. Even at that distance, he could recognise some of them as the men who had laid out the white marker tapes for the monster machines. Behind him, Chipwe and Brunner's good-natured bantering stopped. Just by looking at the men, the beavers knew why they had come. Their intentions were evident in every step they took. For a moment the three of them stood motionless in horror. In the next, they were swimming for dear life back to the lodge to warn Mataama and Nathan and get them away to safety.

'Come on you men! Put your backs into it,' shouted Bourassa. He stood on top of the upper dam supervising the gang heaving on the crowbars below. The men worked hard pushing and pulling from side to side, trying all the time to get better leverage. The dam wall was well founded, however, and was not to be breached so easily. The men strained and cursed and spat on their hands to get a better grip.

'This is going to take all day, for heaven's sake,' grumbled Lopez, resting on his sledgehammer. 'Why don't we dynamite it, same as the trees?' he demanded.

Bourassa scowled. He would have bellowed at them all to shut up and get on with it had it not been for the dogs.

The dogs had quickly lost interest in what the men were doing and had been busy quartering back and forth in the vicinity of the dam. With mounting excitement, they were following the strong scent of beaver. It was Rufus, the big half-wolf Nathan had seen, who was the first to spot the conical-shaped roof of the lodge sticking up out of the water. The other dogs followed in a pack, barking at each other as the musky scent grew stronger.

At the lodge they trod water, momentarily puzzled by the sheer size of it. It hung over them, a massive structure of saplings and hard-packed mud. Somehow, Rufus found the determination to scramble up on top of it. He barked at the other dogs and challenged them to follow. The beaver smell was overpowering by now. It stuck to his tongue. And Rufus knew there were live beavers down there, deep inside. He sensed their presence. He could hear them. He could smell their fear. He sat down, put his head back and howled in triumph.

The men heard him and realised what he was telling them. They stared at one another in rising excitement then with a roar of delight, they left the dam and began to wade waist deep through the water towards the lodge.

The sound of Rufus's howling paralysed the beavers. It filtered down through the lodge into the living chamber where they were huddling round the under-water entrance. It was a horrible cry, a call for blood, and the naked menace in it lifted the hair from their backbones. It was the shriek of nightmares. The dreadful reality they had all heard on the early morning air countless times before and ignored. Now they were about to become the prey.

The growling and whining of the other dogs seemed to be all round them. The beavers looked at each other, their fear now tangible. Nathan leapt into the hole at the entrance and almost at once scrambled back into the lodge. The water was full of confused and threatening sounds. Mataama tried to hurry the twins into the furthest corner of the sleeping chamber at the very back of the lodge. Then just as frantically, she scampered back.

Rufus's howls grew louder. Beyond the noise the dogs were making, there came a surging, splashing sound as if a large animal was threshing about. With it came the sounds of human voices. 'Men!' whispered Brunner. 'They're here. Outside.'

There was a sharp crash overhead. Human voices were suddenly everywhere. The water in the entrance surged backwards and forwards, splashing on to the earth floor of the lodge. Some of it splattered Chipwe, who leapt back as if he had been scalded. The water began to slosh to and fro.

There was a further sharp crash, another and then another as the pickaxes dug into the walls. Soon there was a good deal of dust inside the lodge which made the beavers sneeze and rub their eyes in irritation

Great flakes of mud plaster fell on top of them. More noises came from above. Horrid crashes and ripping sounds. The splash of water outside became more violent.

For the men above, it was becoming a frustrating business. Hacking away at the lodge while standing waist-deep in recently thawed water was rapidly cooling their enthusiasm. Attacking the lodge from above with pickaxes was a more comfortable exercise but just as hard work as the initial assault on the dam had been. Lopez dropped his sledgehammer and clutched at his wrist. He cursed. 'It's like concrete!' he shouted.

Bourassa waved away the mosquitoes that were arriving in droves, attracted by the smell of human sweat. He looked at his watch and what he saw there decided him. They had already wasted half the morning trying to dig out these wretched little animals and at this rate, they'd be here all day long. Worse still, he was being made to look foolish. Some of the men were beginning to grumble and complain loudly about the futility of what they were being asked to do. One of them, a big strapping farm boy almost as tall as Bourassa himself, was becoming a nuisance. His caustic remarks were being greeted with laughter. It wouldn't be long before he started questioning the orders he had been given.

Bourassa decided it was time to assert his own authority once more. He lashed out with his boot and kicked the man backwards into the water. He surfaced choking with pain and fighting for breath. He was no longer an immediate problem. The others looked uneasy but made no attempt to meet the boss's eye.

'All right you men!' Bourassa shouted and motioned to Lopez to stand close by. 'So what's the problem?' he challenged. 'Just a little exercise, a little bit of cold water, and you people start moaning and playing up like a bunch of kids.' He glared round. 'What's the matter? Can't take it?' He waited then shook his head in contempt. 'Anyone want to leave?' No one made a move. No one challenged him. Bourassa smiled.

'So here's what we'll do,' he said. 'Go get the explosives box, Louis,' he ordered Lopez. 'We'll blow these beavers to kingdom come!' A genuine cheer greeted his remarks. 'Now all I want you men to do is dig me a hole so I can stuff the charge in. Do you think you can manage that?'

They continued to cheer and set to with a vengeance.

After a further ten minutes, a hole of sorts had been punched into the side of the lodge, half a yard above the water level. Bourassa inspected it critically. He pushed his fingers inside and thrust them from side to side to check the dimensions. He gave a grunt of satisfaction and motioned to the men carrying the red box. He opened the lid and selected a single stick of dynamite covered in brown paper. He looked round. 'The rest of you get clear,' he barked. 'Go wait the other side of that dam. And keep your heads down when I shout.'

He waited until they got clear. Whatever his failings as a human being, Bourassa was nothing but professional when it came to his job. He had seen too many accidents involving explosives to ever take them casually.

For some minutes, he worked on his own. Deftly he cut a length of explosive and inserted it into the hole. It was about three inches long but he reckoned there was sufficient inside the skin of the lodge wall to do the trick. Next he taped a small primer to the side of the charge. In the top of the primer he attached black and red electric wires. He gave them both a slight tug. They held. Bourassa picked up the box and began to pay out the wires from fixed reels inside.

Carefully he walked backwards towards the nearest bank. When he got there, he put the box down and climbed up after it. There was a large boulder a few feet away and he headed towards it. Carefully, he laid the wires down on the ground and clipped the ends with a pair of pliers. He peeled back the plastic flex. Taking care to keep them apart, Bourassa twisted one length of copper wire round one of the terminals of an electric battery.

'Everyone take cover,' he yelled and waited a further ten seconds. Then 'Standby!'

He touched the red wire to the other terminal. 'Bye bye beavers,' he murmured to himself. There was a sudden rush of flame, a loud bang and the lodge was blown skywards in a huge cloud of debris.

CHAPTER EIGHT

Josh heard the explosion as he was washing up in his kitchen. For a moment he stood there knowing that something was wrong. It was the first explosion he had heard in over a week. He was sure he had heard the men say they had finished their dynamiting. Besides, the direction and distance the dull roar came from were not right. He didn't know quite what it was but his subconscious told him something terrible had happened.

He had heard the men's laughter and their shouts earlier that morning but had given it little thought. Subsequently, he had wondered where they had all got to, for it was obvious that their camp was deserted. No one had even attempted to start up one of the filthy machines. He had been puzzling over it when the muffled bang had come.

He rushed out on to the front porch of his cottage, a cold hand of dread clutching his heart. From the direction of the river, a plume of smoke and brown dirt hung in the air. Like an obscene stain it spread against the blue of the sky. Josh knew instinctively what must have happened, what the men had done. 'No Lord! Oh, please, no!' he cried and ran as fast as he could towards his boat.

Chipwe and Petwa fought for breath. Nothing made sense any more. A moment ago, they had been standing on the floor of the lodge looking upwards and listening. The men and the dogs had gone quite suddenly. They had waded away, making a great deal of noise as they did so. It was as if they had been defeated and were doing it just to cover up their feelings. Bravado or something.

The next, the beavers were struggling to survive in a river that had become the centre of a storm. Waves dashed at each other and broke over the animals' heads in a welter of confusion. They buffeted the beavers from side to side. The water was a churning mass of sand sucked up from the river bed beneath. It scoured their eyes until they stung raw. It got into their mouths and down their throats until they thought they would choke.

It was hard to see much beyond the waves. A thick pall of smoke hung over everything, shutting out the sun. Stones and pieces of wood kept falling beside them in the water. They bumped together and clutched each other round the neck. For an instant, they swayed back and forth, struggling to keep their balance. Neither of them could hear anything above the dreadful ringing noise in their ears. They couldn't hear Rufus barking or the whoops of the men. Instead, they saw Mataama paddling feebly, her head turning this way and that. There was blood glistening from a deep red welt across her shoulders.

Chipwe and Petwa took a deep breath and swam towards her. Somehow they each managed to get a front paw under her. She was almost unconscious and in very real danger. Left to float on her front, she would sink face down in the water and almost certainly drown. With a huge effort, they turned her over, shielding her head as best they could. What next? Through shifts in the smoke they could make out the shattered lodge. It had been blown open to the world. There was no going back there.

They manoeuvred Mataama around and struck out together towards the lower dam, supporting her between them. Water, for so long their friend, now contrived to frustrate their escape. It ran streaming over Mataama's upturned face. She spluttered and tried to turn over. Petwa and Chipwe gritted their teeth and thrust deeper. They had no choice. If the men caught them it would mean death. They had to reach the lower dam and get themselves to whatever safety they could find in the calmer waters of the lake beyond. They remembered the old burrow.

Where the men and the dogs had got to was a thought that only began to occur to them as their memories returned. And now another awful thought hit them. What had happened to the others? To Nathan and Brunner? Grimly, they swam on.

Somehow, they reached the dam. Mataama was almost a dead weight by now. Their forearms were racked with barbs of red hot pain from dragging her along. More dead than alive they reached the lower dam and started to pull themselves up its steep side. Nothing they had ever done in their lives before came within a million miles of the physical agony they felt. Yet somehow – only heaven knows how long it actually took – somehow, they pushed and shoved and used their teeth, claws, fingers and elbows and got there.

They wanted to collapse face down on the branches, oblivious of everything but the need to sprawl dead to the world and rest. But they didn't. Perhaps it was Manitou, the Great Spirit of the Wilderness, who put his hands round them and gave them strength. Perhaps it was instinct. Whatever the reason, Chipwe and Petwa left their innocence behind them on top of that dam.

A new force flowed through them. A new strength, the like of which they had never felt before, got them up on their feet, determined to go on.

Mataama had come round. Though weak and injured she could move her limbs. Chipwe went ahead, scrambling down the other side of the dam and helping her into the welcoming waters of the lake. She began to swim away very slowly with Chipwe beside her, encouraging her. Petwa got to his feet and took a last look back at the shell of the lodge. He froze. What he saw there would remain with him all his life.

Close to the rocks on the far side of the river, where the smoke was rapidly clearing, stood Nathan. Behind him, a jumble of grey rocks reached far above his head. The stones were smooth and offered no protection or way out for an animal in peril. In front of him crouched Rufus, rigid with triumph, every muscle bunched with power. For a split second, he seemed frozen as if in a photograph, his belly part of the rock he would spring from.

In a surging burst of movement, he sprang at Nathan, knocking the old beaver over and slamming him hard into the boulder behind. Nathan staggered and went down with the dog on top of him. The animals heaved and scrabbled and fought for advantage. The dog's breath was sour and felt hot on Nathan's eyes. There was froth on the teeth that raked across the beaver's muzzle. Nathan caught one of the dog's ears and bit it, tearing at it. His mouth was full of blood. But his strength was going. He knew that. It was draining out over the ground and the pebbles, deserting him.

He couldn't get his breath properly. But he had to go on struggling, forcing his chin down over his throat whatever else the dog attacked, whatever the pain. The dog's hind leg drove into his stomach. Nathan gasped involuntarily, his head went up for an instant and Rufus bit down deep into the old beaver's throat. His jaws never slackened their pressure.

Soon, there came a silence. Rufus opened his eyes and bit again into the mess around his jaws. He felt a great tremor course through the beaver's body, then stillness. The dog got to its feet and stretched long and hard, feeling the tension ebb away. He felt wonderful.

He paraded up and down the stony bank shaking his head from side to side as the other dogs danced round him. They were making little darts and rushes at the sad, dead bundle he carried in his jaws. Rufus growled at them to keep off. He growled at the men to stop what they were doing and admire him for what he had done. He tossed the body high into the air then picked it up by the scruff. He wanted the men to praise his skill. But they were too busy with their own capture to notice.

Lopez gave a whoop of triumph and held up Brunner's limp body by the tail. He bundled it into an old sack and quickly tied it up.

Petwa stood there chattering with rage. For one giddy moment he almost plunged back in to attack the men, the dogs ... what did it matter! Ironically, it was a shout from Bourassa that brought him to his senses. He had spotted Petwa and was pointing at him. Bourassa grabbed another man's arm to alert him. They had all seen him by now. The dogs were cursed at and kicked to look in the beaver's direction.

Once again, instinct came to Petwa's rescue. He tumbled into the lake, his tail smacking the surface and, in a cold hatred, swam hard to catch up with the others. One bizarre thing kept hammering away in his brain. He had not realised just how small Nathan had been.

Now they were out where the river met the deep waters of Lake Napachokee. Beneath them, the river slid away under the surface. It made a little see-sawing motion that tossed the beavers up and down for a moment, then it was gone. Mataama was beginning to labour and the pace was dreadfully slow. A long way ahead of them, beyond the next headland, was the hidden burrow.

Petwa swam without any conscious feeling. The pain in his forearms no longer bothered him. Nothing was real but the scenes he had witnessed back at the dam. His mind was struggling to come to grips with the meaning of it all. In a brief instant, everything that was familiar and good had been destroyed.

Both he and Chipwe failed to realise they were being pursued. The first they knew of it was when a shower of rocks splashed into the water beside them. The beavers jerked round in disbelief. They saw the men keeping pace with them on the shore and the head of a dog swimming towards them. They dived. But they couldn't stay under for long. Mataama came up almost at once. By now she had lost a good deal of blood. She was beginning to succumb to the warm, floating sensation that had been urging her for some time to relax. As Chipwe and Petwa surfaced alongside and started to tug and pull at her, she wondered if they'd mind playing on their own. She really was feeling very tired.

The buzz of an outboard engine came clearly across the lake. It sounded like a thousand bad-tempered hornets and it was catching up with them rapidly. Something vicious whipped past Chipwe's head and smacked into the water a scant two body lengths away. The crack of a pistol followed. Both beavers ducked. They knew what the sound meant.

Shamefaced, they came back up beside Mataama. If this was how their lives were to end, they would still go on trying to save their mother until their hearts ruptured in the effort. It was all part of the uniqueness of being a beaver. Their instinct made them keep on swimming in the hope, no matter how forlorn, of escaping their enemies.

The dog swimming after them was steadily gaining on them. The boat was going flat out with a great white wave tossing from its bows like some enormous arrowhead.

It must have seen Chipwa and Petwa because it altered course and cut in towards them. It scythed through the water, the bow rising higher and higher almost on top of them, then it was past and a great wash tumbled them over and over. Somehow, they found each other again.

Behind them, Josh hurled defiance at the men on the shore. A stone hit him but he seemed not to be aware of it. He was shouting at the beavers but they couldn't understand what he was saying. Josh called again, more slowly this time. 'Go on beavers. Go on! I'll cover you with the boat.' He stopped when a slug from the pistol hit the wooden gunwhale in front of him in a shower of splinters. It was Josh's turn to know fear.

He gulped and stared at the shattered wood in disbelief. And then the old railroad man saw red! He picked up a stone lying at his feet and threw it with all the strength he possessed at Bourassa. By a miracle it hit him on the shin. 'See here you crazies!' Josh yelled. 'I'm going to Port Henry for help. I'll have you all in jail, so help me, if it's the last thing I do!'

Bourassa, who was no mean judge of men, saw and heard. There was no mistaking the determination in the old man's voice.

'Cool it! Cool it!' he snarled and knocked up the gun in Lopez's hand. It fired again but the bullet went high over the boat. Bourassa spat in disgust and rubbed his leg. All this fuss over a few beavers. The world is going mad. All this environmental rubbish! These same wretched animals had kept his men from a whole morning's vital work. Mr Sekri wouldn't understand, of course, why it had taken so long to get rid of them. There'd be yet another fit of bad temper. Who'd be a construction manager? He should have gone in with his cousin after all and run that bar in Montreal.

Bourassa urged the men back to their camp. As he fumed at them he decided it was about time that Josh Gilpin left the scene permanently, one way or the other.

Josh kept the boat between the beavers and the shore until he was certain that the men had gone. Then he followed the animals at a respectful distance, using an oar over the stern to skull with.

Petwa and Chipwe were hardly aware of his presence. All their concentration was focused on reaching the far headland and the secret burrow. Perhaps it was the sudden reappearance of the men, or it may have been the help Josh gave them, but Mataama seemed for a while to have caught a second wind.

Her eyes were almost closed and her breath was coming in fast and shallow wheezes, but she put her entire being into reaching the burrow. Only at the very end did she pass out, but by this time they were within yards of their goal. They got her ashore and found a smooth rock at the water's edge to lay her head on. Then both Chipwe and Petwa slumped down beside her.

Later, towards the end of the afternoon they dived to inspect the burrow to decide how best to get Mataama in there. Then they took it in turns to stay with her unconscious form while the other went foraging. Finally as the sun began to slide to the bottom of a cloudless sky they woke her and half dragged her to the water. It seemed to take an age to cover the remaining distance. As they trod water above the burrow, both the young beavers whistled as loudly as they could to wake her. She would need full lungs for the dive as the water was deep here. On the second attempt they were successful and all three of them finally pulled themselves up into the burrow and collapsed on a dank-smelling floor.

A merciful Nature took pity on them and they slept where they lay, Chipwe's tail trailing in the water. This was no time to fret about what had happened to Nathan or Brunner. Now there was only oblivion.

CHAPTER NINE

Brunner shrank back in the cage as the dog's head suddenly appeared. Rufus opened his jaws and gripped the wire mesh with his teeth and began to twist it from side to side. He was barely six inches away from where the terrified beaver crouched up against the back of the wooden box the men had made. Bourassa's huge dog stood on its hind legs, fur bristling.

Brunner wrinkled his nose at the dog's scent. He could feel the dampness of its breath on the air in front of him. He could see the red hatred in the dog's eyes and had no difficulty in realising his fate if Rufus broke in. Now he understood the threats the dog was snarling at him. He had been spared this at first when he was still deaf from the explosion.

The men had kept him in an old sack while they knocked the cage together. The dogs had butted him with their heads and urinated on the sack. Then Brunner was tipped into the converted orange box which was hung from a large nail on a fir tree close to the men's campfire.

For the first couple of days the men had come to peer and poke him with pieces of stick. But their attentions were nothing like as bad as the searing headaches he had endured at first. Only the dogs were regular visitors. Now though, Brunner could not hide his fear whenever they came. There was a hatch on one side where the cook pushed through a tobacco tin full of water and scraps of food each day. Someone had written on the front of the cage in ink 'Big Brian's Zoo'.

Brunner wondered what had happened to the others. He decided they must all be dead. He would never see any of them again. Hungry, cramped and dirty, he cowered at the back of the cage.

'Mr Neary, what are you doing down there?' Miss Dent called. At the bottom of the wooden stairs that led from the editor's office to the archives, Jack Neary was poring over old, faded copies of the Port Henry Times Clarion. He hardly heard her. All his concentration was centred on the yellowing page on the table in front of him. A solitary light bulb dangled, spilling shadows across the walls. Jack had banged it with his head a couple of minutes ago, when he had stood up abruptly in excitement. He had found what he was looking for – that tiny echo of memory old Josh Gilpin had set him remembering.

His finger had raced down the columns of old news. The momentous events and community doings that might still be as vital today as they were then. Not that life had really changed so noticeably over the past ninety years, Jack noted. The Eagle Tavern, then known as The Prince Albert Hotel, had been the scene of a brawl between a couple of fur trappers and a survey party from the Osagwa, Namchuck and Port Henry Railway Company. The leader of the railway men, Black Bruce Kemp, had been thrown in the town jail to cool off.

According to the newspaper, Port Henry was divided over the coming of the railroad. The mayor and the business interests were strongly in favour, claiming it would bring prosperity to the area and help in its settlement. The churches were stridently opposed, the evils of drink being only one of several condemnations used. The majority of townsfolk were undecided.

'Mr Neary! May I remind you that we have a newspaper to put out tonight!' Miss Dent had clambered down the narrow stairs and now stood facing him. 'You haven't even begun your editorial. Do I have to tell you again?'

Jack stared ahead thinking hard. He barely noticed her. Around the walls, great bundles of old unsold editions had been stacked one on top of the other, right up to the great pine beams that ran the length of the room. There was a pleasing smell of dust and old newsprint. Jack now knew beyond doubt that he was on to something. A casual remark by the old man, together with his own nose for a story had sent the world spinning on a totally different axis.

He grinned at Miss Dent and for a moment had a wild notion of throwing his arms around her. 'Read this Miss Dent.' He motioned her to come round beside him instead.

'Mister Editor, do I have to remind you for a third time,' she began in her most severe manner.

'Hang it woman!' Neary snapped in quite uncharacteristic brusqueness. 'Read this, will you! And then tell me if we aren't sitting on the biggest story this town has ever known.'

Miss Dent had every reason to be affronted. She began to draw herself up to her full height but something in the editor's voice stopped her. Instead, she gave him a quizzical stare, adjusted her spectacles and peered at a headline entitled: 'Mayor and Council Agree Railway Expansion In Return for Land Commitment'.

She began to read the report of the deliberations and eventual legislative action passed by the city fathers. When she had finished, she went through it again reading the key passages out loud in rising excitement. Neary watched her, the grin on his face stretching even further.

'Looks like we're going to need some sharp legal advice, Miss Dent,' Jack told her. 'So who's the best lawyer in these parts?'

Miss Dent thought for a moment. 'Thorburn's the one to go to', she reflected. 'He's mean. He's nasty but he knows his stuff. And,' she added 'he's not afraid of anyone.'

'Then go get him, Miss Dent!' Jack cried. 'Before it's too late.'

The beavers lay huddled in the darkness of the burrow. They packed together for reassurance clutching at each other and burying their noses in the familiar scent of each other's pelt. But there was little real comfort to be had. The air was dank and smelt alien to them. It had a mouldering, rotting tang to it that perfectly matched their misery. Earth fell from the tree roots above in sudden little runs. It slipped into their nostrils and mouth and the more they used their forepaws to scrub it out, the deeper it went. Then they would snuffle and snort in discomfort.

For the first couple of days after those terrible events, they had just lain there quivering with fright and exhaustion, occasionally whistling to themselves. All sense of purpose, of activity, even of going out to feed was obliterated. Their lives had only one focus. There was one reality that dwarfed everything else. How to stop the dreadful ringing noise in their ears. The jarring, endless discords that raced round inside their heads until they yelped in frustration and pain. They were all quite deaf.

Later, as the fever grew and swelled inside Mataama, drenching her fur in sweat, the noise in their ears began to weaken. As it did so, they felt their energy returning. The young beavers heard Mataama groan.

The wound in her shoulder was caked with dried blood. It smelt foetid. When they sniffed it, the flesh was hot on their nostrils. Mataama whimpered to herself in a way they had never heard her do before.

They tried to groom her but the fever defeated them. Her pelt had become a mass of wet curls. The heavy, flat tail lay motionless. She lay with her eyes half open, breathing in quick, shallow gasps. A fly had somehow got into the burrow and it sucked greedily at the wound.

They tried to catch it with their paws and kill it, but it buzzed away each time. It was the fly that decided them. They plucked up courage and eased their way out of the burrow, back into the hostile world outside. Chipwe led the way.

Under a brilliant, star-packed sky, they swam and dived and regained their identity. The water felt like silk on their parched coats. It flowed through their fingers in moonlight streams. They tried to eat it and bite at its loveliness, all the time chattering with new found glee. They chased each other's tails and performed acrobatics in celebration, half-mad with pleasure. The water washed the dirt and discomfort from their fur and some of the pain from their minds. Then, it brought them back to reality.

They trod water and talked together in the silent, passive way beavers do. Mataama needed help. She must feed or die. This would be their first priority. Next, her wound should be properly cleaned. Then they thought about Nathan and Brunner and the men, the flash and the world caving in on top of them. And they had to duck down under the surface to hide from these thoughts. Afterwards, while Petwa collected water weed,

Chipwe climbed the bank above and went in search of the special grass that heals sick animals.

Soon, Mataama began to eat again. As she gathered strength, the wound, now clean and cooled by the lake water, started to heal. The night came when, after taking infinite care to check there were no traces of man, they swam together for the first time as a family. Mataama was still lame in one hind leg and swam awkwardly. She used her tail as a scull to balance herself.

They knew that they were all preparing themselves to leave the safety of the burrow and return to their proper habitat. Flowing water had to be dammed and new lodges built. It was as simple and as eternal as that.

Mataama, Chipwe and Petwa did not dwell overmuch on recent events. They filed away their recollections of what had happened in that part of their memory best described as 'experience'. It would be imprinted there, ready in an instant to spring up and warn them of danger. This is not to say they did not talk about Nathan or that they had forgotten Brunner. They mourned them both and were sad at heart. Mataama missed Brunner in particular for deep, but as yet unformulated reasons.

Human beings marvel at the love dogs give them and tell true stories of dogs waiting at their master's grave for years, hoping he will return. What they may not know is the fierce loyalty that exists between beavers in the same colony.

So when the crows eventually spotted the twins out foraging, they swooped and screeched and fought with each other to be the first to give the beavers the news.

Chipwe and Petwa dropped the branches they had been dragging and sat up on their haunches in bewilderment, staring at the birds whirling overhead. The crows landed heavily and ran towards the beavers in their usual awkward way, squabbling and pushing and beating each other with outstretched wings.

It took some time before Chipwe and Petwa were able to piece together the news. But when they realised Brunner was still alive, the beavers stood rigid for a while then began to tremble with emotion.

Slowly, they turned to look at one another to confirm what they had just heard. Finding the same answer, they went mad with delight, rolling over and over on their backs then scrambling up to chase their tails, barking and whistling like animals possessed. They sparred with each other, boxing and slapping good-humouredly at the other's face before dropping to their feet and rushing at the crows snarling in mock ferocity.

The crows took off in a cloud of flapping wings delighted with the beaver's reaction. Below them, Chipwe and Petwa dodged in and out of the trees racing one another in their turn to give Mataama the news.

It was getting on for late evening and nature was caught in a no-man's-land. The sun had long since slipped its way down the western heavens. It was that in-between time, when the day birds were beginning to close an eye and think about bed while the night creatures were still waking up, having a good stretch and discovering how hungry they were.

Across the surface of the lake, insects sank lower, attracted by the reflection of the sunset. A few late feeding trout hurried upwards and jumped for them. In the swamp above where the top dam used to be, the frogs were facing another episode in what was fast becoming an epic saga of horrendous proportions. They were experiencing a trauma of their own. For the past few nights they had woken to find the river swirling past. None of the frog elders could remember a time when the river had ever been in such a hurry to join the lake. It made feeding distinctly uncomfortable. Undignified too, what with having to hang on to something pretty tightly before taking a decent sized bite at a water weed or a young lily pad.

Frogs are temperamental creatures. Their tastes tend to the flamboyant. While they try and order their lives around the 'live and let live' principle, the reality of frog life is one of frequent emotional outbursts and loud vocal disagreement. An aroused frog, a frog with a grievance, can quickly become seven ounces of undiluted, hopping rage.

Right now, the frogs were on a very short fuse. Most of them were tired, hungry and conscious of a loss of individual dignity because of this new water flow. All this rush and splash and these strong currents seeking to whirl them away from their homes and places of entertainment were totally unacceptable.

They had held the biggest protest meeting anyone could remember the night before. The one planned for this evening promised to be even better attended and far more acrimonious. A swelling chorus of croaks could be heard even now. By midnight it would be deafening. But it would be all to the good if the beavers finally got the message.

It was obvious that the beavers were to blame. It was sheer irresponsibility at this stage of natural development, for them to let their dams fall apart. After all these countless generations of evolution, why wasn't it possible to create some form of inter-species co-operation? It really was too much!

Chipwe and Petwa said their goodbyes and slipped quietly into the lake. They swam for a good five minutes under water, careful not to leave any mark of their passage which other animals might see and note. With especial caution they surfaced, their heads hardly making a ripple on the darkening waters. Around them, they could feel fish still swimming, hopeful of snatching one last fly before night finally fell. The fish would glide past then, realising the beavers were much bigger than they were, they'd give a panic-stricken flap of their tails and disappear down between their hind feet.

There were other less pleasant sensations on that long night swim to the beach below Josh's cottage. Unpleasant memories from way back when they had been very small beavers. Recollections of bad dreams about Grancha, the monster pike, perhaps swimming somewhere below them. Chipwe and Petwa instinctively swam closer together.

It seemed an age until the glow of the men's bonfire appeared in the gathering darkness. The crows had been right about that, at least. A little further on and much lower down in the gloom, they picked out the gleam from the solitary oil lamp Josh burned in his cottage.

A breeze hesitated, then started to blow out from the shore. It brought with it the scent of men and dogs and the warm, choking smell the machines made. At first, they felt almost sick as memories and panic came racing back to warn them. Taking even more care they tested the night air but could find no trace of Brunner. Some time later, they heard the sound of men talking. There was a great deal of laughter and the odd shout. The men's voices sounded hoarse. The beavers swam on, approaching the lakeshore at an angle.

They were getting very close now. Chipwe felt the tension buoying him up and wondered if his brother was feeling the same. Ranger must be chained up on the front porch of the cottage, he decided. He could hear the squeak the chain made as the dog padded up and down. Ranger was restless, still not used to this new indignity inflicted on him since of the arrival of these dreadful men.

Noiselessly, Chipwe and Petwa glided into the shallows where the water felt warm. They were keyed up for action. In the past few minutes, they had seen and heard the men come out of a large cabin. Strong smells of food had followed them. One of the men carried something that screamed and wailed and which must surely terrify every living creature around, thought Petwa. But none of the others paid it any attention whatsoever.

Chipwe nudged him and indicated the loom of Josh's boat tied up alongside the landing stage. Hardly daring to breathe, they sank into the water and dived under the boat to emerge in a silken movement among the weed-covered supports beneath. They were in enemy territory! Both of them released a pent-up breath.

'Got far to go, Beavers?' came a loud voice almost in their ears. Petwa bit his tongue so hard he could still taste the blood an hour later. Chipwe just about jumped out of his skin and cracked his head against a wooden pile. The sound of the splashes they made brought Ranger to a sudden halt. He growled.

'Oh don't mind him any more!' said the same voice. 'He's harmless now he's tied up. We just saunter past and tease him, poor dear. Just to show him he's no longer top dog, if you see what I mean.' The animal laughed. By now, the beavers had picked out the pair of large, round eyes gazing at them from what seemed to be upside down. Suddenly, a large raccoon clambered down from the wooden planks of the jetty and squatted on a beam beside them.

'I'm Riki,' he said. 'I say,' he continued, giving them no chance to get over the shock he had given them, 'are you by any chance related to the beaver the humans have stuck in that frightful cage thing?'

'That's Brunner,' said Petwa licking his sore tongue on his paw.

'How is he? Is he all right?' Chipwe hissed, not in the least amused by the stranger's behaviour.

'Not too chipper, actually,' the raccoon replied. 'Not surprising, I suppose. I mean, they're trying to feed him on all those scraps they leave. Quite unsuitable for a beaver of course. And then, there are those ghastly dogs. They take it in turns to stand nearby and bark threats about what they're going to do to him. Most unnerving, I would have thought.'

'Where is he now?' demanded Petwa.

The raccoon studied them. It put its head on one side and stared at them. 'Do you two have ideas of rescuing him?'

'Once we know how the land lies, yes. Of course,' said Chipwe.

Riki considered this and started to rub his chin. 'Won't be easy,' he commented. 'You see, the men hang his cage from a nail in a tree at night. I'll show you if you like,' he offered. 'But it won't do you much good, will it?' He looked at them and giggled. 'I mean' he said, 'whoever heard of a beaver climbing a tree?' At this he put his paws across his middle and began to shake with laughter. 'Oh dear!' he apologised, rubbing his eyes with strong, clever fingers. 'I didn't mean to be rude. Do believe me. But I never could resist a joke.' And he went off into peals of laughter.

'Can't you help us?' said Chipwe looking at Riki's powerful hands. 'I hear there's not much raccoons can't find a way of breaking into. And a cage shouldn't be too much of a problem, would it?'

Riki thought about this. 'Yes, you're right there,' he agreed. 'I suppose it could be done, technically speaking that is. The door's only kept closed by a catch and a piece of stick. And as far as I know, beavers and raccoons don't have any bad blood between them – well not that I'm aware of.'

The others agreed.

But Riki hesitated. 'Only problem is,' he said thoughtfully, 'I don't want to do anything to set the men against us. I mean, it's pure heaven for all us raccoons with them being here. You should see what they leave for us to eat. Why, I'm getting positively sleek these days.'

'Maybe' snapped Petwa. 'But don't you also forget, raccoon, they're the same men who'd kill you right now whether you were scrounging or not.'

'Probably use your pelt for a fur coat or something,' added Chipwe with a similar flash of irritability.

'And they have the cheek to call us brutes,' Riki sniffed.

'Oh come on!' urged Chipwe. 'It'll take you no time at all. Look, there's an animal's life involved.'

'You don't understand,' Riki said after a little sulk. 'I'll have to talk it over with the others. It should be all right but, well, there's bound to be some who'll object. I'll do my best for you.' Then seeing the expressions on their faces, he added quickly, 'Look! You beavers have your own rules too, don't you? I mean, I daren't do it if the others disagree. They'd drive me out and we raccoons aren't very good at surviving on our own. I'd be eaten by something really brutal almost at once.'

The beavers said nothing. They were lost for words at such selfishness.

'Just give me a couple of nights,' Riki said 'and I'll meet you back here. I'm sure it'll be fine.'

'Can we see where he's being kept?' Chipwe asked.

'What, now you mean?' Riki sounded astonished. 'Oh ... all right then,' he replied grudgingly. 'But don't blame me if anything goes wrong.'

They followed him, taking care to keep a good four body lengths between each other. This is standard beaver practice as it gives would-be predators a minimum target. Riki paused for a moment to spit at Ranger before moving along again at a quick trot, keeping well hidden in the shadows. They could hear the old man's voice behind them calming Ranger. Then they were climbing uphill.

Petwa was amazed. It had all changed so much. Most of the trees had gone and there were wide level terraces of earth when once they had stood. Huge ruts made, he presumed, by the giant machines, criss-crossed one another heaving up vast heaps of dirt. Some were quite difficult to climb over and their paws sunk deep into the sandy soil. He noticed the half-built cabins standing overlooking Josh's cottage. They stood beside a wide, newly made track. Dumps of other pre-fabricated house parts were piled high at regular intervals along it. There was an overpowering smell of pine resin and a scent he had not come across before, creosote.

Riki slowed and indicated the long cabin they had seen the men come out of. 'That's where they eat,' he murmured, 'And here's where we feast,' indicating the row of dustbins to one side. 'I'm tempted now, as a matter of fact, just to have a quick snack.'

'Oh please, raccoon,' cried Petwa. 'Just show us where Brunner is, please!'

Riki made a clicking sound with his tongue. He shook

his head in self-commiseration. 'I'm getting a real softie in my old age, I am,' he said. 'Come on then! It's not far. But be careful. Keep your eyes on me!'

Past the cookhouse they padded. They could hear a man singing or moaning to himself inside. Petwa couldn't decide which. Up the rising ground to a ridge where the raccoon hunched down on the ground and peered cautiously over. When he was satisfied with what he saw, he beckoned Chipwe and Petwa to join him. As the beavers came up, he put a finger to his lips and pointed.

In a clearing below, the men and their dogs were sitting around a roaring fire. Flames shot up from it. Sparks were singeing the lower branches of a small clump of Douglas Firs. A sudden roar of laughter almost sent the beavers scuttling away in terror. 'Keep still!' the raccoon ordered. 'What's wrong with you?' he hissed, furious with them. 'I need to make sure the dogs are all down there.'

While he studied the group round the fire, Chipwe found himself looking at a shadow on the trunk of a huge tree. A shadow that didn't seem to flicker or twitch like the others. It was about a metre and a half above the ground which was an odd place for a shadow to stay. Only it couldn't be a shadow, he decided. It was fixed. It was an object of some sort. He realised in the same instant that there could only be one 'object' like that. It was Brunner's cage!

He nudged Petwa and pointed to it then grasped his brother's ear, holding it very tightly indeed. Petwa gulped down the sick taste that had risen in the back of his mouth.

The raccoon began to sidle along a massive wheel rut which led down and away from the immediate glare of the fire. Soon they were in total darkness again, squinting to get their night vision back. They scurried along for a good hundred metres towards the tree where Brunner's cage was hanging. They huddled in a patch of long grass for a council of war.

'No sense going any further until that fire goes down and they all go to sleep,' said Riki.

'But we've got to let him know we're here,' hissed Chipwe in desperation.

'Look,' said the raccoon. 'I'll tell you what I'll do. I'll come back much later on and cheer him up. Now, I can't say anything fairer than that.' He peered at them in the gloom. 'If you beavers want to take the risk,' he shrugged an expressive pair of shoulders and rolled his eyes. 'Well, that's up to you. Anyway, I'm starving. You know the way back. Try not to get caught for my sake. I have a reputation to think of. I'm off!'

'We'll see you in two night's time. Don't forget!' called Chipwe. But by then, Riki had disappeared into the darkness.

With their hearts in their mouths, the beavers approached the tree. It was a venerable old fir with gnarled roots that spread out across the ground on all sides, affording good cover. There was also a low, stunted bush in front of it which screened it from the men's bonfire. With pounding hearts they were sure every dog for miles could hear, they inched their way around to the bush. They lay still, listening, watching for any sign that they had been seen.

An age crawled past before either of them felt sufficiently reassured. They began to tremble at the terrible urgency of the situation. They had to know if Brunner was still alive. They must comfort him as best they could and keep his spirits up.

'Brunner! Brunner!' they whistled, softly at first then with rising recklessness. 'Brunner! Oh Brunner!'

On the far side of the fire, Rufus opened one eye. Something had disturbed him. What? It was not his master's shout of laughter. Rufus knew every cadence of Bourassa's voice. Besides, this had not been a human sort of noise. He strained his ears for a moment longer but whatever it had been, it was not repeated. He sighed to himself and went back to his doze.

Petwa had gnawed a long stick from the bush. With infinite care, Chipwe reached high and rapped at the bottom of the wooden cage. He went on doing so until something, someone in there began to scrabble to its feet. A voice, a low, sad, miserable voice muttered 'Who's there? What do you want? Who are you?'

Chipwe took a deep breath and fought to get his feelings under control, for all their sakes.

'Brunner! Don't call out whatever you do. It's us. Petwa and me, Chipwe!'

Brunner was thunderstruck. For a long moment he froze, then a wild elation overcame him. He seized the wire mesh in front of him and tried to bite through it. He shook it and pummelled it with his paws in frustration. Beside Bourassa, Rufus raised his head.

'Be quiet Brunner! For pity's sake,' the beavers hissed at him. 'Or we'll be captured too.'

Rufus couldn't bear it any longer. He didn't know exactly what it was but there was something happening out there, beyond the flames and the heat and the comfort, that needed his attention. He got up, stretched, and ran a tongue over sharp teeth. A large hand grabbed at his collar and a bone was thrust at him. Rufus wavered. But the smell of marrow was compelling. It wouldn't take long to demolish it, he decided. He settled back down with the bone between his front paws and cracked it open with the first bite. In any case, he thought, it was probably only another of those raccoons.

111

Unaware of the drama that was being played out beside the fire, Chipwe and Petwa raced lakewards. The only creatures to see them go were Ranger and Josh. Josh was sitting on the top step of his porch, stroking Ranger's head. Above him, like some gigantic stage effect the moon had risen with all the brilliance and suddenness of summer. The ground was bathed in a cool blue light.

A beetle was half way across the sandy patch in front of the cottage when the two beavers raced past. The sand from their hind feet buried it in a sudden avalanche.

The man scratched his head in bewilderment. In all the years he had lived by the lake he had never, ever seen anything as strange as this. Ranger barked once, twice, then thumped his tail. Which was another mighty strange thing as well, come to that, Josh reflected.

CHAPTER TEN

A thin rain covered the lake. It was a cold, spiteful rain, an unwelcome visitor from north of Hudson's Bay with no patience with the summertime. Very soon after it had settled on Lake Napachokee, it had bled the colours from the trees; reduced the lake itself to a sullen grey and the surrounding hills to gloomy, sepia tones. Later that morning, the wind had joined it, pressing down even harder, whipping at the water with sharp-edged raindrops and sending bad-tempered waves pounding on to the beach in front of Josh's cottage. It discovered the construction workers huddled round an earth grader and fell on them with glee. It lashed their faces like many fine strands of barbed wire. Beneath its onslaught, the men complained and grew sulky. They whiled away as much time as they could standing still inside their oilskins, sucking at their roll-up cigarettes.

Bourassa had left to go to Port Henry some time before the rain had started. He wasn't expected back much before early afternoon. Lopez, who was left in charge, was no great lover of conditions like these. So the men hung round, looking sufficiently busy to give the section heads no reason for leaving the site office, with its steamed-up windows, to come and re-direct them.

As is so often the case with humans, the weather directly affected Josh's mood. Earlier, just after dawn, he had walked out under a sky that was rapidly clouding over with a thin, scummy covering. Even at that time of the morning, one of Bourassa's side-kicks had seen him and had come down from the cookhouse to bar his way. In none too gentle terms, he had seen to it that Josh returned to the cottage. Ranger had set up a furious barking when this happened and Josh had had his work cut out to prevent the animal getting kicked again.

Ever since Sekri's men had arrived, Josh and Ranger had been virtual prisoners, allowed only the freedom of the cottage and its immediate surroundings. It had got steadily more oppressive. Ranger had to be kept chained up. Whenever Josh had tried to venture further afield, an unsmiling hulk of a man had turned him round and on two occasions, had frog-marched him homewards.

After the terrible events of the blowing up of the beaver's lodge and the shooting incident, Josh had not dared take his boat out on the lake for fear of what he might find on his return. He know the time could not be long delayed when he would be unceremoniously forced out. He had already packed some personal papers and a quantity of food in his old army kitbag. It stood up against the door jamb ready for him to pick up and take to the boat when the moment came. There had been one major confrontation since he got back from shielding the beavers. That same evening, Lopez had driven a bulldozer directly at the cottage, swerving away only at the last minute but knocking Josh's forty-gallon water barrel high into the air. It hit the ground and caved in.

The old man was also depressed by the progress the men were making. Each day, the wooden landing stages for the future marina grew closer and closer to his little beach. Yesterday, they had dumped a whole load of fresh timbers and deck planking right beside his jetty, in anticipation of what was to be built there. Already, a dozen or more of their holiday homes had sprung up immediately above his cottage.

Last night, after a lot of thought and some talking to Ranger about it, Josh had drawn the curtains very carefully, stood on a kitchen chair and reached along the top of the venerable mahogany wardrobe that had once been his grandmother's. He had lifted down a very old, but serviceable shotgun. He hadn't handled a sporting gun for close on fifty years, not since that occasion when as a young man, he had gone out 'hunting' for the first and last time in his life.

He held the gun with hands that trembled slightly. He felt its weight and gauged its power. Josh stroked its cold barrels and wooden stock, knowing that, as a last resort, it might be some form of protection in the frightening world that had come to the lake.

The twelve bore cartridges were in a box in the bottom of the wardrobe. He took the box out and put it down on the kitchen table. He hoped the cartridges would still fire after such a long time.

Later that morning, as Josh peered out into the grey damp, something inside him rebelled. He broke open the old cardboard box and thumbed a handful of cartridges into the pocket of his waterproof. Hardly knowing why he was doing it, except that this might be the last time he would enjoy freedom, he stepped out on to the porch. The rain lashed down and there was no sight nor sound of anyone.

He was tired of all this Prisoner of Zenda business. If he was to be evicted from the place he had spent so many years growing to love, then he would go with his head high and not like some whipped cur. He bent down and unchained Ranger. 'This might be the last time we do this, old fellow,' he warned. 'So, remember ... enjoy it.' To the accompaniment of a peal of thunder they went out into the rain. Josh took a deep breath of air that smelt of bracken and old pine needles and freedom. They walked round the shoreline, up over the rocks that formed the headland and back towards the men's camp. Underfoot, boots squelched and left sharp patterns in the soggy earth. In the undergrowth, the spider's webs sagged and refused to gleam. Ranger, after an initial leap of excitement, had by the end of the first kilometre huddled closer to Josh. He was getting fed up and critical of his master's urge to stay out in these hideous conditions. Men wore more than one skin – something they always forgot to consider. One of the worst things about being a dog was putting up with this human urge to go out in terrible weather. So, with a less than enthusiastic Ranger plodding on behind, they passed close by the men's cookhouse where the dog gave a brief display of alertness. But the man in there was fast asleep and his stove long since grown cold.

At the end of the building, a fifty gallon drum of paraffin leaked unnoticed from a split in a faulty seam. It had done so for weeks now and it was just under half full. The earth beneath its stand was saturated and a thin black trail drained its way down the hill towards the lakeshore. The cook used the fuel to top up the lamps he put out at night to keep the raccoons away. It was a miracle they hadn't upset any. As a fire risk, it was spectacular.

Josh and Ranger trudged on through dripping undergrowth. The scent of the intruders was everywhere, which depressed Ranger still further. He had already been driven off his own patch by these new creatures so picking up the scent of Rufus on a low bush made his hackles rise. What could be more miserable than this, he thought to himself?

Brunner watched the man and his dog appear over the ridge. He sat slumped in a corner, feeling cramp pains creeping up his hind legs. He couldn't stand

116

upright as the roof of the cage was too low. It was barely wide enough for him to turn round in. It was filthy and Brunner had accidentally knocked over the cigarette tin which held his drinking water. He was half-frozen from fear, lack of exercise and this driving rain that lashed at him through the wire netting. Chipwe and Petwa's visit seemed a lifetime ago and he wondered whether or not he had actually dreamt it. Still, there had been a raccoon who had also appeared. He had brought some nuts and Brunner had eaten them, shells and all. So perhaps it had all happened as he imagined.

Brunner didn't know much about Josh but recognised him from the description the others had given. He watched as the man stopped to turn a bottle over with his foot and study the label. The dog stood behind him waiting. Brunner's teeth chattered. All of a sudden he made up his mind. His reserve, his beaver pride, even his animal caution at the sight of a human with a gun and a dog, couldn't hold him back any more. He pressed his muzzle to the wire and shouted for help.

It was thanks to Ranger, to rain-lashed, cold-pawed, wretched Ranger that real help was forthcoming. Josh did hear a faint chittering but if he thought anything of it at all, he put it down to either a bird or the chipmunks. It was the bedraggled Ranger who understood and sympathised with Brunner's plea for help.

He ran ahead, barking. Josh shouted after him in surprise but Ranger was off. Over the sodden remains of the campfire he raced; past the strong smell of the other dogs to stop at the foot of a tree. He stood on his hind legs and looked back over his shoulder. That was when Josh noticed the cage hanging there. For a moment he stared at it, puzzled. The next, he had broken into a clumsy run and was panting hard by the time he reached the tree.

Josh looked inside the cage, his face puckering in disbelief. He saw the beaver huddled inside. He looked at the cage again and automatically noted it was barely the animal's length and not much longer. He saw the scratches in the bark where Bourassa's dogs must have stood barking, a few inches from the terrified animal inside and he took in the lack of drinking water and the untouched pieces of meat.

'You poor old chap!' was all he could trust himself to say. Carefully, he undid the catch on the outside of the door, talking all the time to Brunner in a quiet, reassuring voice. He held the door slightly ajar while he let the beaver get used to his presence. On no account did he want to frighten it. He talked about the lakeside chase, how he had protected the beavers in the water, how he had escorted them to an over-hanging bank. And about the bullet that had hit his own boat.

Carefully, he put his hand on Brunner's back and began to stroke it. Brunner flinched away. He couldn't help it. Josh's hand froze. The man stood there for perhaps five minutes, quite motionless. He prayed silently that Ranger would not leap up and scare the animal still further. The beaver was in a terrible condition, its eyes dull and its pelt matted. It was very weak and any sudden shock could just stop its heart.

The warmth of his hand seemed to relax the beaver eventually and Josh continued to tell him how two beavers had raced past his cottage in the moonlight and plunged into the lake.

Perhaps it was this or the gentle sound of his words, but Brunner accepted him and after a little while longer, licked his wrist. Josh cried intense tears of love as the beaver let himself be picked up and held close to the surprising warmth of the man's strange, furless body. Almost at once, he fell asleep. He remembered the dog barking but it was a friendly sound. He felt like a cub again.

CHAPTER ELEVEN

Brian Bourassa's day began well. True, he was still livid after getting back yesterday to find the door of Brunner's cage open and no sign of the beaver. That was really annoying. He had been planning on having some fun with the animal and then having him stuffed by a taxidermist he had heard of in Port Henry. That beaver would have looked really good in the den of his house. Perhaps with a little brass plate underneath and a date to remind him of the details. On second thoughts, he had toyed with the idea of presenting it to Mr Sekri himself with 'The Lake Napachokee Project' or some such title tastefully engraved on the plinth. There was a snag to that one, though, as he remembered – his boss hated all animals and couldn't even stand a dog coming up to him.

That reminded him to put Rufus and the others on a chain next time Mr Sekri visited. There was no point upsetting the boss again over something as stupid as a few dogs, for Pete's sake! He brooded over Brunner's disappearance for some time. The beaver couldn't have escaped on its own. Some other creature or more likely, some person, must have been involved in freeing it. His own men wouldn't have dared to, besides, they had been looking forward to a bit of sport every bit as much as he had. No! It had to be that weird old Gilpin guy. Yes ... the more he thought about it, the more sure he became. Interfering old fool!

He whistled to Rufus and set off on a tour of inspection. He thrust his hands deep into the pockets of his donkey jacket because even in late June it is still quite fresh first thing in the morning in the Northlands.

As he trudged along, he decided that something had to be finally done about Josh Gilpin. So far, Parker Properties had been pretty good to him. In Bourassa's experience, unbelievably so. They had let him continue here long after he had been given notice to quit. Bourassa didn't know why the corporation was being so lenient. That was up to Mr Sekri. When he had asked him why the old man had not been evicted, Sekri had told him it was a matter of politics.

'All the local idiots up there think he's some kind of folk hero. So we've got to be seen to be caring and humane, at least until we've got the job up and running. Then we can bulldoze his shack into the lake for all I care, any time we want. Get cracking, Bourassa! You're costing me money taking all this time to get things done ...'

However, as Mr Sekri was frequently out of the country on business deals, he had given Bourassa power to intervene directly if Josh impeded the actual progress of work. That gave him an idea. A brilliant idea. So much so that Bourassa put a fresh matchstick between his teeth and thought about it in more detail. He leant his back against a tree and watched Rufus and the other dogs run after fresh scents.

As Bourassa saw it, Josh Gilpin had just declared war on the project. He was interfering with the progress of the job by freeing that beaver. The men had been looking forward to all sorts of fun with it and maintaining the worker's morale was high on the agenda of any efficient manager. A happy work force got the job done quickly. Anything that detracted from that cost Mr Sekri a whole load of dough! And Gilpin had deliberately sabotaged the men's welfare. Bourassa smiled at the realisation. His mother often told him he was the brains of the family. Perhaps she was right. Women usually were.

He thought some more. Of course! It was right under his nose. Josh had also been trespassing on company property when he freed the animal in the first place. Cool, brazen disregard for another person's legal rights. Diabolical! It was a blow at society itself. He'd go into town that same day and make an official complaint to the RCMP. Mr Sekri would like that. It made what would happen next kind of legally justifiable and inevitable.

On top of all this, Bourassa reminded himself, the project was back on schedule. The men had done well these past couple of weeks. Now was the perfect time to take the gloves off and blow this old pest clear away, once and for all.

Bourassa felt very happy. He quickened his pace and headed down to the lake shore where he surveyed with pride the three brand new landing stages reaching out into the lake. They'd each take ten boats a side and this was only the first of the three marinas they'd be building. The others would follow soon. They looked good. Like something from a holiday brochure. He turned round and admired the row of white painted cabins looking out over the lake. The men had done well. Heck! They deserved a party. The development was looking just like the architect's model he had been shown. It didn't take too much imagination to picture the place by August, already full of people having a good time, motor boats roaring away from the docks, water skiers hanging on behind. That sort of thing.

Bourassa let his enthusiasm take over. A couple of fast food places over where those beavers had been messing it up. A couple of hundred tons of concrete to flatten it all out, lots of neat little trees planted along the pathways.

Wow! It would be really something. That's what he liked about working for Mr Sekri. It was satisfying. Gave a man a real sense of achievement.

On the way back, he stopped off at the cookhouse. The cook was hard at work getting breakfast ready. He shoved a plate of sausages at Bourassa. He wore a singlet and a gold cross on a chain round his neck. A cigarette burned on the counter top beside him.

'We're going to have a party tonight, Philip. Can you barbecue some chickens, that sort of thing?'

'Sure, Mr Bourassa,' the cook replied. 'Is no problem. I fix.'

On the way out, he bumped into Lopez. 'Hi guy!' he greeted. 'It's time for action, Louis. We'll have some real fun before the night's out.' And he told him what he had in mind. They both laughed.

'Sure thing, Brian,' Lopez called after him.

The crows saw it first as they flew over to the far side of the lake not long after dawn. It hadn't been there the night before and it was spreading out from the burrow the beavers were staying in.

They circled overhead and discussed what it might mean. They swooped down low almost to ground level, then folded their wings, stalled and landed heavily. For a moment they studied their surroundings with beady eyes that missed nothing.

They hopped to and fro for a while digging their cruel, heavy beaks into the grass to help them hear whatever it was going on below. They heard faint scrabblings and once the sound of a stone clinking on another one. A faint sneeze followed by a distinct splash.

The muddy stain on the surface of the lake gave a quiver and began to widen. Satisfied, the crows took off in a noisy chorus.

The mystery was solved. It was just the beavers extending their burrow.

'How are you feeling?' Chipwe asked. It was wonderful to be up here in the forest, cutting sticks to support the walls and roof of the new chamber they were constructing.

'The leg's a bit stiff still,' Mataama replied. 'But it'll be fine for tonight,' she reassured him.

'It's a long swim,' he warned. 'And you need to be really fit to help us get Brunner back. We can't have two of you needing assistance. We just couldn't manage.'

'I'll be all right. I promise you,' she said. And she spoke with such authority that Chipwe let the matter drop.

They worked for a long time in silence.

'Shoulder all right?' he asked suddenly.

Mataama nodded and spat out a piece of bark she had been chewing. 'Time for me to relieve Petwa,' she said in reply.

'The thing that really worries me,' confided Chipwe, 'are the dogs. I mean, what do we do if they pick up our scent? It's easy for raccoons. They can climb out of the way. We can't.'

Mataama rubbed the fur on her flanks over and over again in short, circular movements. Then she washed her face. She did it to give herself composure.

She was still larger than Petwa and Chipwe and, of course, their mother. Secretly, the whole idea of going to bring back Brunner and having to trust animals as notoriously unreliable as raccoons frightened her.

That was why she had insisted they enlarge the burrow way beyond what had already been done. It was the only way she could cope with it all and hide her fears under the guise of action. It had not been easy to get them to agree to it. In the end, she had to give Petwa a fierce nip. For a moment she thought he was going to defy her and bite back. The fur on his face had puffed up in anger but she had hissed him down. She knew she still exerted power over her two cubs but it was clear that it couldn't last for very much longer.

She found herself needing Brunner and thinking about him as if he was already back. For that reason alone, she knew she would have to go out and fight to get him back where he belonged.

Brunner did not wake up at once. Something warm was tickling his nose. He twitched but it would not go away. He rubbed at it with his paw but it persisted. In the end, he opened his eyes, only to be dazzled by a brilliant shaft of sunshine that was chiding him for not being up and about. He rolled over and, still half asleep, began to wonder where he was. The air was full of strange and exciting scents; new wood and fresh air certainly, but above all there was an overwhelming smell of man and dog. Man! He sprang up in fright. His head all of a sudden felt muzzy and he sneezed not once but several times.

He heard a human voice calling and then Brunner remembered a great many things. Some of them were good. He sat very still and looked around him. Wherever he was, it was a very big chamber. The roof seemed to stretch upwards for ever.

'You're all right. You can stop looking so worried. No one's going to hurt you,' said Ranger, who was sitting in a shadow under the open window. 'Josh says you've been pretty ill. How are you feeling?'

The beaver looked over at him in surprise. Dogs were never normally that friendly, so it was clear that Ranger was making a big effort to sound reassuring. 'Funny though,' said the dog, looking at him in a surprised way, 'I never knew beavers caught colds!'

Later, after he had slept a great deal more, Brunner learnt more of what had been happening from both Ranger and the kind human whom Chipwe and Petwa liked so much. The man Josh had come into the room very slowly and laid some recently cut aspen branches on the floor in front of him. Afterwards Brunner fell asleep. He wasn't well, though he knew he would be better quite soon. His animal commonsense told him he was safe here until then.

If anyone had told him before this that he'd ever feel safe in the company of a man and a dog, he would have thought them mad. It was a bit smelly though, and he couldn't get rid of that odd, sweet flavour in his mouth. The branches had been a generous and thoughtful gift but why oh why, did humans have to smell so strange? He drifted into a deep sleep.

'Just let me check on that,' said Moira Burt, the female assistant from behind the counter at Mason's General Store. She gave the huge man in front of her a tantalising look. Unfortunately, Bourassa chose that moment to pick at a tooth with a cracked fingernail so the effect was lost on him. However, Moira Burt had already made a favourable impact on the rugged project manager. He liked small, blonde chicks like this one. Heck! He had a reputation from Elk Jaw to Klondyke Falls to maintain.

Bourassa leered at her. Not that he would have considered it as such. He gave the sort of cool look any powerful, real man would give any attractive female. It took the form of a slow grin and his putting his head on one side, to show he was really a great big kitten at heart with sensitive feelings beneath it all.

He was feeling very pleased with himself. Less than one hour ago, he had had a conversation with Mr Sekri that had been nothing short of masterly. First, he had given a glowing report on the progress that had been achieved. He spent some time elaborating on the potential money-spinning atmosphere of the place with the cabins and marina in place. Sorrowfully, he then related how Josh was becoming an implacable foe and was physically interfering with the well-being of the development. He had been forced, in the face of much provocation, to formally complain to Officer Robinson.

Mr Sekri, who took the call in the back of his stretch limousine, listened, assessed and decided. 'If we're as well advanced as you tell me, then ... well ... perhaps. But Bourassa, make it look like an accident! I'm on the point of selling it on. So be careful. Runaway vehicle, that sort of thing. Understand?'

Bourassa smiled at the recollection and extended it to include Moira Burt.

'So you're wanting twelve cases of beer ... a crate of redcap whisky and three big tins of baked beans,' she confirmed.

'Got it in one,' he agreed in mock admiration.

'You boys having some kind of celebration tonight?' Her smile was unmistakably friendly.

'Well now, we might just be at that,' he agreed. 'The boys out there have done a great job for me. I just want them to know how much I truly value their loyalty and hard work.'

Moira Burt was very impressed with the speech. She admired masterful men. There weren't that many in Port Henry. 'Oh Mr Bourassa,' she gushed, feeling strangely moved. 'I knew it the moment you came to this town. You're a real inspiration!'

Bourassa chuckled and picked up her unresisting hand. He kissed it with a ponderous charm. 'At your service, Miss! Perhaps one day soon, you might like to be my personal guest and let me escort you over our entire new development.'

She looked at him with shining eyes. 'Oh, I'd love to. And I can even meet my friend who lives out there. You must have seen him. He's an old timer called Josh Gilpin. Though, now I recall, he's not been in here for some weeks. He's still around, isn't he?'

Not for an instant did the smile leave Bourassa's face. He did, after all, have a reputation from somewhere to consider. Instead he said evenly, 'If Mr Gilpin's there at that time he'll be more than welcome to come along.'

After that he wheeled his purchases away on the store's biggest trolley. He had just finished stowing the cases of beer in the boat, when he became aware of three men looking down at him from the jetty above. He straightened up, shielding his eyes from the noonday sun. 'Hi!' he called. 'Can I be of assistance in any way or are you guys looking for a job?'

Thorburn, the lawyer, a thin little man in a shiny dark, suit bent down towards him. 'Are you Brian Rene Bourassa, employed as project manager for Parker Properties Incorporated?' he questioned.

'Say, what is all this?' Bourassa replied belligerently. He looked at them more closely and noticed the big man in uniform. 'Gordon! What are you doing here?'

RCMP Constable Robinson felt unhappy and not a little confused. He was an ambitious man and saw the Lake Napachokee project as the best thing that had happened in years. He had also taken a liking to Bourassa at their recent meeting. All these big city fellows he knew had influence. So now, he shuffled his feet in embarrassment.

Robinson licked his lips and cursed under his breath. Not for the first time he reflected that it was tough being a cop. He had been summoned at breakfast that morning to go round and see the mayor who, for what it's worth, was Miss Dent's younger brother. Over pancakes and a mug of coffee, the mayor had explained what was to happen and Robinson's own part in full. 'Just do your duty to the community you serve, Gord, and I'll make sure it doesn't go unnoticed at the highest levels in the county.'

A sharp kick on the ankle from Thorburn brought him back to the job in hand. With evident reluctance, he took the papers from the lawyer and cleared his throat a couple of times before serving legal notice on Bourassa, as the legal representative of his firm, to cease all commercial activity, further development planning and contractual obligations forthwith until the case came to court.

When he had finished reading the document out loud, he clambered down an iron ladder until he came level with Bourassa, who by now was red with rage. 'You didn't tell me this before you sneaky, two-faced son of a polecat,' Bourassa spluttered.

'No trouble, eh,' Robinson hissed back and thrust the papers into the other's open hand. Bourassa grabbed at him but Robinson was surprisingly agile for such a big man. He shot back up the ladder and laid a meaningful hand on the revolver holster at his belt. 'Get out of town and stay out, Bourassa,' he shouted. 'If I catch you back here, you'll be locked up!'

Thorburn called down to him. 'You and your company have illegally damaged and in many instances totally destroyed, the property of the legal owner, namely, a Mister Joshua Gilpin. My client here,' he indicated Jack, who was busy taking photographs, 'has started an action against...' But the rest of his sentence was drowned as Bourassa yanked the engine into life and surged away in a cloud of blue exhaust.

He stood all the way back, his expression unchanged. Gilpin! That doddery old man! He was pathetic! But he was making fools of them all. All this 'legal owner' nonsense. What the heck was that supposed to mean? The smartest lawyers in the country worked for Parker Properties.

And that journalist fellow! He was behind all this. The press were always trying to make trouble. Together they had stuck a knife right between his shoulders. He, Bourassa! The best known hard hat in the development business. Perhaps they were trying to get him the sack stirring up the dirt like this. Mr Sekri had warned him it was political behind the scenes.

He leant forward and pulled a bottle of whisky from its crate. He took a long swig and then another. He began to roar and shout. Gilpin, that dried up old spider! Gilpin! A born trouble-maker. Well, he'd get even. Make no mistake. He'd grind them all under the tracks of a bulldozer!

Mr Sekri would be furious. He'd blame him and probably sack him because of this. Bourassa knew his boss too well to have any illusions on that score. He expected nothing less. 'Well,' he thought to himself, as he gunned the engine and headed towards the beautiful marina that he was building so lovingly, 'well, he'd take that old buzzard with him if it was the last thing he did!'

Ranger was bored. He was bored with not being able to go anywhere or do anything. Ever since yesterday morning's marathon walk in the rain, Josh had put him back on the chain. Worse still, he had kept him on a lead of all things when they had slipped out for a quick walk last night. Josh himself had stayed awake for most of the previous night, sitting just inside the porch door, a shotgun across his lap.

Josh had explained to him a long time ago that these strange men would shoot him if he strayed and Ranger, after a couple of exchanges of hostilities with Rufus and his pack, believed him. All the same, ever since he could remember he had had the run of all the land round here. He had chased rabbits and chipmunks, squirrels and raccoons with total freedom. So why had things changed, he wondered for the hundredth time. And, more importantly, what was Josh doing about it?

Ranger thought his master was behaving in a spineless sort of way. He just hung about the place like a grey ghost, terrified to leave the cottage. The trip they had taken when he rescued the beaver, was their first daylight expedition in a long time. And what, for goodness sake, was the fun in going out in a downpour like that! What was the point of being a human if you couldn't do what you wanted to do, when you needed to? Come to that, he thought moodily, there wasn't much point in being a dog in these circumstances either.

He yawned and settled his head down between his paws. Gosh! He was even getting bored with sleeping. He watched an ant running for dear life over the wooden step. Might as well have been born one of those, he decided. At least no one chained them up. On second thoughts, he'd have like to have been a skunk. Now that was what he called fun! If he'd been born a skunk, why, he'd be able to go exactly where he chose, men or no men. There wasn't an animal born who'd take on a skunk.

Ranger began to enjoy a pleasant daydream in which he was a skunk and king of all he surveyed. He took on whole gangs of shouting men and hysterical dogs and with one threatening lift of his tail, he put them to flight. He would even warn those yellow machines to leave.

Then suddenly he found he wasn't concentrating any more ... something was wrong!

He opened his eyes and listened hard. There it was again. Chanting! Men's voices shouting something over and over. He could hear Rufus barking at the other dogs but he couldn't quite make out what he was telling them. They were heading this way and moving quickly. Ranger sat up and growled. There was a prickly feeling of unease round his collar. He realised that it had been unusually quiet all afternoon, as if the men hadn't been working. That thought occurred to him when he heard the sound of one of the monster machines suddenly roar into life.

Ranger was on his feet. He could sense intuitively that something bad was going to happen and that both he and Josh would be involved. He barked in earnest, hurling threats at whatever it was on the other side of the ridge.

Josh came out of the door and stretched. 'What's the matter, old fellow?' he asked. 'Horse flies bothering you?'

'Listen!' willed Ranger. 'Just listen to what's coming for us. And unchain me while you're about it.' He looked up at Josh and bared his teeth wide. Not far away a machine gave a grating, grinding bellow.

Josh heard it too. He listened calmly at first and didn't seem to feel there was anything untoward until the moment the monster lurched over the hill. There was something about the speed it was making and the crowd of men running alongside waving their fists and cheering, that shocked Josh into action.

He dashed inside the cottage and was back almost at once with the shotgun in his hands. He held it to his shoulder and Ranger saw his body shaking. The dog didn't hesitate. This was bad. He sprang out at the advancing machine as far as the chain allowed. Sure enough, Josh understood and to his relief called him back to free him. Together they watched while the bulldozer came straight for them, the tracks slipping sideways in its rush.

The massive blade began to lower. Josh gesticulated with the gun, warning it away, but after a few more seconds it was obvious the machine wasn't going to stop. He fired one shot over the top of the driver's cab. Nothing happened. The machine was only yards away. Ranger could see Josh had left it too late. The gun fired a second time and the great burning eye of the machine shattered into a thousand pieces. The machine slewed to one side, spraying earth and stones from its tracks. A plume of exhaust belched upwards. For a split second longer, Josh held his ground, then, hurling the shotgun at it with all the strength he could muster, he turned and ran with Ranger barking alongside him. Behind them came a stupendous crash as the bulldozer ran straight into the side of the cottage.

Somehow, they got the boat clear of that terrible place, Josh almost falling over the dog in his panic to cast off, start the engine and push them clear of the landing stage. The engine coughed, threatened to cut out, then caught. There were men wading out after them, their mouths black holes in their faces as they screamed abuse. Stones began to splash around them.

The bulldozer gave an impatient roar and took a second run at their home. The house swayed then began to buckle. The wooden pillars at each end of the porch snapped like twigs. The chimney fell through the hole that was starting to open up in the roof. With a crash that could be heard for miles, all that was left of Josh's great grandfather's cottage was a splintered pile of matchwood and memories. And, Josh presumed, one dead beaver.

Thirty minutes later, the crows circling overhead, almost incoherent with excitement, saw another amazing sight. Josh stopped the boat close to the steep overhanging bank where three other beavers had headed all that time ago. Nothing was said and the man just bowed his head. After a pause, the boat resumed its journey down the lake and was lost to view.

A passing stranger wouldn't have thought there was anything remarkable at all. Just an old man in a boat with a dog standing silently in the bows.

CHAPTER TWELVE

It was a black, black night. The lake surface was
perfectly still, almost as if it were holding its breath,
waiting for something momentous to happen. There were
not even the usual water noises to break the silence.
No sudden chuckle of water moving over a stone; no
wavelet playing with the sand, even the ducks deep in
the reeds were quiet. Just a heavy dark cloak of stillness
that covered water, swamp and land alike.

The blackness was a perfect cover for the beavers'
progress. They swam on the surface in a loose arrowhead
formation, with Chipwe leading, Petwa and Mataama
immediately behind him on either side. They had decided
to travel this way to ensure no one got lost in unfamiliar
waters. There was no animal to see them go and no
creature marked the spreading ripples made by three
small heads. They dug deep with their hind legs into
the waters of Lake Napachokee and the powerful motion
began to build a strong, disciplined rhythm that bound
them even closer together. The surge of water under them
inspired confidence in their purpose and unity. It
became an insistent drum beat, a call they would
follow wherever it might lead them.

With the smallest of swirls, Chipwe altered direction
and headed for the deep channel between One Tree
Island and the rocky shore. They passed through, barely
able to make out the approaching land, but aware of the
change in temperature in the water below them. Even
Red Claw, the great owl, failed to spot them, though he

sensed their presence many feet below his nest in the dead tree. He sat taut with interest, head to one side, puffing out his feathers in concentration while his huge eyes glared into the night. Perhaps he caught something of their sense of purpose, for he shivered and launched himself from the branch and flew off on silent wings.

Still the beavers swam on. Another mile and yet another, and then Mataama could see the glow from the men's camp, exactly as they had told her she would. Out here, the noise the men were making sounded very close. Mataama shivered. Her throat was dry. Chipwe hissed at them to close up, then he altered direction slightly and led them in towards the shore.

The fire gave a sigh and sank lower on to its bed of hot ashes. It crackled and flared for an instant before the flame flickered and went out returning to a ruddy glow. A couple of the men were still awake, having a last drag on a shared cigarette. One of them bent and threw another branch on the fire. Most of the others were asleep either in their trailers or sprawled on the grass by the fire. Rufus lay gorged on chicken and sausage. He was happy, growling in pleasure every now and then and dreaming the dreams that make a dog smile.

From the middle of a bramble bush, Brunner watched him. He stayed rigid, gazing down at the firelight and the leaping shadows it made. For the beaver, it had been a nightmare ever since the first shattering crash had pulled him from a deep sleep. He had started to run after Josh and the dog only to find a huge crowd of men almost on top of him. He knew he had no chance of racing past them to the lake, even had he been in full health.

He stared at them in horror, then felt the impact of the second bulldozer assault. He scuttled into the furthest corner of the room, dodging falling timber and roof slates. More by luck than judgement, he had managed to reach the old kitchen table as the chimney went straight through the floor beside him, splintering open the planks.

Brunner dared not move until the darkness came. He had to fight to stop himself sneezing as the dust and flakes of white paint drifted over his coat like fine powder snow. He knew the dogs were near. He heard them snuffling round, sometimes getting quite close. But no one came to disturb the debris piled up in a high pyramid over the table.

He waited until he heard the owls setting off on their night's hunting before he made his move. Then he eased himself as quietly as he could down on to the ground and picked a path through the destruction. It was pitch black. He felt the dampness of the lake on his muzzle and turned towards it.

From the darkness ahead came a sudden crashing. It was a man! Brunner's nostrils were thick with dust. He had had no idea the man was there. The man lurched towards him, singing loudly. Without pausing to think, Brunner went for him. The man, who probably never even saw him, gave a frightened yell and went over like a skittle. The bottle he was holding smashed on the ground beside the beaver's head and the raw spirit splashed up into the animal's face. Brunner's eyes closed shut a fraction too late.

The liquid burned and reduced him to immediate blindness. Its stink was everywhere. Totally disorientated, Brunner ran for cover ... away from the lake.

At a soft cry from Chipwe, they closed up until they were almost shoulder to shoulder. They swam very slowly, searching the blackness for Josh's old landing stage. The marina came up suddenly, almost in front of Petwa. He pushed into Chipwe, warning him away. That gave them the bearing they needed and soon they neared the jetty, their noses picking out the pleasant smell of weed. They slipped under the pilings and lay there, getting their breath back. After a little, the wave that marked their passage rippled on to the sandy beach in front of them. Then it was gone.

'Goodness me!' came the voice. 'This is all most impressive.'

There was a squeal, a loud splash and sounds of a struggle in the water. Mataama gritted her teeth. What on earth was going on, she wondered? They heard Chipwe's frantic whisper.

'One more wriggle out of you, raccoon, and I'll hold you under for ever!'

Petwa stared ahead, frozen with horror. How could the men and the dogs not have heard all the commotion? It would ruin their plan before they had even got ashore. And all because of this stupid raccoon.

Chipwe held the animal by the scruff and increased the pressure of his fingers. It began to snuffle and whimper. He clamped a cold, wet hand over its mouth. A very long five minutes passed for the beavers waiting motionless in the shallows. Gradually the tension lessened. Perhaps they had got away with it after all. They began to breathe more easily and move their cramped limbs.

Still firm in Chipwe's grip, Riki whispered sulkily, 'If you'd only asked me first, instead of all this strong arm stuff, I'd have told you.'

'Told us what?' snapped Petwa.

'The humans are all up at the fire. That's what you might need to know, I imagine,' the raccoon replied sarcastically. 'Can't you hear them? Or are you as deaf as you are inconsiderate. They're having a fine old time, aren't they. Eating, drinking and singing.'

'And the dogs?' Chipwe demanded. 'Where are the dogs?'

The raccoon peered at him. 'They're up there with them. All those lovely bones and things. I say,' he added. 'Your beaver escaped, didn't he? The human rescued him. But now the men have driven him away so your beaver's hiding somewhere, isn't he?

'You're a deceitful creature,' said Chipwe. 'I don't believe a word of it. You agreed to help us to get him back. And that's exactly what you're going to do.'

'Hiding! Did you say he was hiding?' Mataama interrupted. 'But where is he? Oh please help us, raccoon, please.'

All of a sudden, Riki wriggled and slipped out of Chipwe's grasp. He swarmed upwards on to a guardrail well above them. 'Find him yourself,' he spat. 'Talk about rudeness! I've got a good mind to tell the dogs. You just see if I don't.' He ran along the jetty and they heard him jump down on to the sand and begin to scamper away.

'Quick! We've got to stop him getting away,' hissed Chipwe. 'Mataama!' he ordered. 'Please stay here. We'll come back for you. Don't worry, we won't be long. Petwa! Come on. We've got to stop that raccoon or we're done for.'

They chased after Riki. The raccoon's scent was all round them and they had no trouble following him along the lake shore. They raced round some of the new holiday cabins and almost caught him hiding beside a pile of planks but he dodged away, wrong-footing them with a sudden change of direction.

The raccoon headed uphill towards the glow of the men's fire. The beavers with their short front legs were at a disadvantage and Riki drew further ahead. Now he was some yards in front. He threw a glance back over his shoulder, then scrambled up a tree.

'Right! You asked for it this time,' he spat from a branch high overhead. 'I'm really going to tell the dogs!'

He ran along the branch then launched himself into the middle of another tree. The tree swayed under his weight and sprang back again as the raccoon jumped for the next one. Petwa and Chipwe followed as best they could but Riki was soon out of sight in the darkness.

It seemed to take forever before Brunner's eyes were normal again. To be blind and surrounded by enemies who would have no compunction in killing you is a nightmare experience for anyone to have to endure.

To Brunner, it had seemed like some weird dream. It was happening to him but it didn't feel real. He kept stopping to sit and listen, straining his ears for any indication of danger, while his eyes smarted and filled with tears. He felt totally helpless. He blundered into trees, fell between boulders, crashed through undergrowth – for all the world like an injured bear. Perhaps, he owed his survival to that!

His worst fright came when he found his eyesight coming back. He opened his eyes and discovered he was crouching in the middle of a wide open patch of freshly cleared scrub with an earth-grader parked a mere fifty metres away.

Now he lay silent and watchful, trying to decide what to do. The scent of men and their dogs was everywhere. It lay on the cool night in so many greasy layers. Their noise and laughter filled his ears. Below him, in the hollow he knew so well, they swayed and shouted and stood close to the blazing fire. Brunner lay with his belly hard on the ground and waited.

*   *   *

Big Brian Bourassa drained the bottle with a flourish and threw it into the middle of the fire. It gleamed for a moment then sank into the ash. He belched and rubbed both hands over his stomach.

'Feeling good, Brian?' Lopez called across to him.

Bourassa considered the question with all the seriousness of a drunken man. He began to nod and a wide smile spread across his face. He nudged the man beside him and held out a hand for the bottle the other was holding.

'Louis,' he slurred. 'I'm feeling great! Really great. Best day of my life.'

'You sure got rid of that Gilpin guy, Brian,' Lopez agreed.

'Better believe it,' said his boss slumping into a sitting position. He took another swallow, the liquid spilled out over his chin. 'Better believe it,' he mumbled and passed out.

Beside him, Rufus stirred, stretched and looked around. The wind had changed direction. It carried with it different scents, intriguing smells that hadn't been there before. It was time for a walk. He got up and was aware of the other dogs watching him, waiting to react to whatever he ordered. But Rufus was sleepy from the heat of the fire. He growled a single, brief command for the others to stay where they were while he padded up the slope towards the bramble bushes.

Brunner watched the great dog approach in disbelief. A whimper began to form in his throat. Rufus was sixty yards away and below him, but his intention was clear. A late night prowl, nothing more and nothing less.

He was not suspicious. That Brunner could tell from the way he walked. There was no obvious purpose in his stride. As Brunner watched, he stopped to yawn and the beaver saw the great jaws open to their fullest. All the while, Brunner faced a dreadful dilemma. If he stayed where he was Rufus would pick up his scent. That was only a matter of time. On the other hand, to move now would risk the dog hearing him.

In the hollow below, the few men still awake started to sing. The sudden noise distracted the dog who stopped and looked back over his shoulder. Brunner needed no further encouragement. He had to get back to the safety of the lake and a shift in wind had shown him where it lay.

He backed out of his cover as quickly as he dared. Not waiting to see how successful he had been, he raced away as hard as he could. It was a joy to be running towards safety and Brunner put his heart into it. He bounded over long strips of cool grass and burst through the low-lying tangles of blueberries, which tried to trip him and hold him back. He kept up speed until he reached a massive boulder standing out against the night sky, where he lost valuable time deciding which way round to go.

He followed a stream bed because it gave excellent cover but found the rocks and pebbles an increasing hazard. Beavers are not made to run over rough ground for any great distance. The pads on his feet had grown soft since his great cross-country trek and the sharpness of the stones cut and bruised them. He began to limp and run in a curious skipping motion.

Behind him, close to the top of the slope, Rufus stiffened. The dog wrinkled its nose and all at once became alert. He sniffed at the air just above the ground. There was no doubt about it. It was beaver scent and a very fresh one at that.

He investigated further, pushing his way into the bushes. A beaver had been lying here; its warmth was still rising from the earth. The overhanging branches were trapping it. There was no mistake. Rufus gave a growl and began to cast round to find where it had got to.

Down on the lakeshore, Mataama was beside herself with excitement. At first she had obeyed Chipwe's order to stay close to the water. She waited patiently for what seemed an age after the others had taken off after that wretched raccoon. Before long, the noise and the presence of the men began to unnerve her. She began to run backwards and forwards in short rushes, quartering the ground. Anything was better than just waiting.

It was while she was casting round on the slope above Josh's ruined cottage, that she picked up Brunner's scent. There was no doubt about it. She knew he had been there earlier that same day.

Torn in her loyalties, she didn't know what to do next. In the end, she stood upright and began to whistle as urgently as she could into the night. Someone had to hear her!

Brunner knew the dog was following. Ever since he had slipped and fallen in the stream bed, he had known it. His euphoria evaporated. He was no longer a beaver running towards freedom and friendship. He was once again a hunted animal, pitting his wits against a better equipped predator.

He couldn't hear anything above the pounding of his own heart and the lungfuls of night air he was sucking in. Inside his head, the sound of his panting became a roaring noise. Mechanically, he plunged on. He almost went head over heels when his forepaw caught in thick bracken. It tugged at him, forcing him to slew to one side before he burst through. He licked at his lips which were cracked and dry but there was no spittle on his tongue.

And all the time, he knew the dog was gaining on him. The darkness ahead was mesmerising. He daren't look back in case he slowed or fell while doing so. He had to keep going, driving his legs on to where the lake must be. To where the water lapped in unconcern but which would accept him without question.

And then, a man's hut showed up ahead and as he momentarily caught his breath in shock, he heard Rufus's snarl – very close. Brunner veered sharply to his left. There was no reason to suppose it was a better way of avoiding the inevitable but there might just be something. He might be able to protect his back and at least face his enemy. That would give him some possible fighting chance. He skidded around the far side of the cabin.

Facing him was a row of dustbins surrounded by rotting vegetables. Brunner barely had time to take in the scene before he was upon them. A large raccoon was sitting astride one of the bins rocking it backwards and forwards to tip it over and get the lid off. It glared at him with huge eyes. Brunner was aware of a light on top of a table and at least four other raccoons staring at him and beginning to shriek in panic.

He tried desperately to avoid them, but his hind feet slipped on the mess they had made and he cannoned full tilt into a tall wooden stand nearby. There was a massive thud as the paraffin barrel rolled off and crashed to the ground. Then it went rolling and bucking down the slope, gaining momentum with every second. The split in the seam opened wide and the fuel spurted out. It went lurching on down until it fetched up on a tree stump very close to the first of the holiday cabins. The paraffin continued to spill.

Rufus, racing after the beaver, knew he was gaining with every stride and by exactly how much. He could anticipate to the second the moment he would be able to launch himself and bring it tumbling down. The muscles in his powerful hind legs bunched and then powered him a further foot closer to the despairing Brunner.

Rufus sensed the beaver's frantic weave almost in the instant the thought first crossed Brunner's mind. Rufus had allowed for it. As Brunner ran to the left, Rufus was right behind him and still gaining all the time.

Only a few moments now separated them. But then, as Rufus rounded the side of the hut there came a sudden burst of barking and the hollering of men's voices from the direction of the campfire. The dogs had found a raccoon and were chasing after it. It only distracted Rufus for a split second but that was just long enough for him to run full tilt into a rolling dustbin. He tried to jump over it but a raccoon got in the way. Rufus barked in rage.

One of the watching raccoons knocked over the lamp the cook had left as it scrambled to safety. The lamp rolled off the table, hit the ground where the safety glass smashed. The flame inside seemed to hesitate for a moment then it licked at the ground and with a whoosh a wall of fire blazed up.

Within seconds, flames were burning fiercely along the far end of the hut. The raccoons fled, panic stricken. Rufus yelped in shock and ran into the darkness before rolling over and over trying to beat out the flames that crackled at his chest. A twisting finger of fire raced down the slope, feeding on the spilt fuel, greedy to find its source.

Brunner saw the flames and heard them roar. They were after him, he was certain. Where Rufus was, he had no idea. He knew the dog was somewhere behind him, immobilised by this greater enemy which could run at a speed far greater than any animal he had ever known.

The flames were coming for him, raking towards him with long fiery claws. They were catching up so quickly. It was like a nightmare. He couldn't seem to move his legs. Then he heard a beaver whistle over to the side. His legs were rooted to the spot. Now the ground beneath was holding him back. It was heavy and sandy and wet. He staggered into the lake and fell flat on his face.

From somewhere, whether it was close or far away he didn't know, he heard another whistle. Then another. He opened his mouth to respond but it filled with water. It was all a dream. It had to be. There were dogs barking nearby. They were getting closer. Brunner began to scrabble at the sand, trying to kick himself clear. Then he was surrounded by his own kind, scents he recognised, and they were pulling him out into deeper water and safety.

Behind him, the barrel exploded with a loud thump. Trails of burning liquid ran in all directions. A flame flickered then took hold. Soon, the white paint began to blister and turn yellow. The flame grew hotter and spread. It separated into two flames. The wood was dry beneath the cheap paint and the cabin was engulfed within twenty minutes. The one next door took even less time to burn.

CHAPTER THIRTEEN

Mr Sekri slammed the phone down and swore. He got out of his chair, came round to the front of his desk and lashed a kick at a small table that held a vase of flowers. The water drained into the thick pile of the carpet, leaving a stain behind. A dozen yellow carnations fell in a soggy heap.

Outside the huge office windows, the lights of the city blazed into the night. Advertising signs flickered their messages in eye-catching reds and oranges and greens across the front of vast buildings. Tail-lights from a thousand cars gleamed and the muffled roar of traffic provided an ever-present backdrop.

Burns, the lawer, went over to a cocktail cabinet and mixed them both a drink. 'We always knew it was a gamble,' he said in a mild voice as he handed Mr Sekri a glass. 'That restrictive covenant was as clear as a bell to anyone who bothered to read all the way through.' He paused, assessing the other man's reaction. 'The law is the law, I'm afraid. And where it applies to land its constraints are for all time. You know that.'

He broke off as Mr Sekri began to bang his fist on the desk top, slopping his drink as he did so. 'Sure I know all that!' he shouted. 'What do you take me for. Some kinda dummy? What I want to know is how this fellow Neary got in on the act and how come he knows so much and how come we didn't buy him off!'

The lawyer made a placatory gesture and waited till

the other had finished a further bout of rage. 'Neary found out about the covenant from the newspaper archives,' Burns said. 'So he discovered that Gilpin was the outright owner not just of his house but most of the lakeshore as well.'

This remark further incensed Mr Sekri. He struck his brow with the palm of his hand. 'And that great ape Bourassa bulldozed the place down. So tell me some good news!'

'It could be a whole lot worse,' Burns reasssured him. There was a pause.

'Look,' Burns said in a crisper tone. 'I've been talking all day to this Thorburn lawyer, the one acting for Neary and the old man.'

'So what's the latest?' Mr Sekri interrupted.

'Here's the deal. And it's OK, believe me,' Burns told him. He got up and began to pace up and down in front of the massive desk. A note of triumph crept into his voice.

'If we rebuild Gilpin's house and restore the land as much as it can be to what it was, then they'll take no further action. There'll be no claims for damages, destruction of property, nothing!'

Mr Sekri was impassive.

'How long have we got?' he asked.

'They want us out in five days,' Burns told him gazing down on the city below.

Mr Sekri sat back in his chair with his hands crossed on top of his stomach. He thought for a while.

'What's their real price?' he demanded. 'How much to buy them off, Burns? A million ... more? Level with me. That place is a goldmine. You know that.'

The lawyer shook his head. 'I tried all that stuff. I even went up to a million and a half but it didn't wash. Men like Neary and Gilpin prefer principles to cash.

Don't ask me why. I've met people like them before. Strange, but that's how they are.'

He leant over the desk facing Mr Sekri.

'Do you agree to their terms? Do we have a deal?' he asked.

To his surprise Mr Sekri did not answer at once. 'Didn't animals come into this somewhere?' he mused.

Burns made a face. 'Bourassa reckons raccoons knocked over the lamp. They caused the fire, he says.'

At the mention of Bourassa's name, Mr Sekri became decisive again. He sat upright. 'OK. So here's what we do.' He spread his hands on the marble desk top. 'About Gilpin's shack. Agreed! Build it. Use what's left of the cabins. Get Bourassa on to it first thing tomorrow.' And for the next couple of minutes he rapped out his orders.

Later, when Burns got up to leave, Mr Sekri said something strange, almost as if he was confiding to himself. 'Remember I had those beavers killed off? And now some other animals have done all this damage up there. It's almost like a revenge, or something.'

Burns was amazed. He had never heard Sekri talk this way before. For a moment the remark quite threw him off balance. 'We were fully insured,' was all he could think of saying as he closed the door behind him.

It was the crows who brought the news. News that was so unexpected that no one could believe it until they had seen for themselves. The news also came in the nick of time.

A few days after Brunner's dash for freedom and the long night swim back to the burrow, all four beavers were crammed together in the living chamber, silently deciding what to do next.

At first they had slept, overjoyed to be together again. But for the past twenty four hours they had been facing up to the fact that they couldn't stay where they were for very much longer. Beavers find it impossible to be inactive. The lake called to them to come out and busy themselves building dams and living the life Nature had equipped them for.

As soon as Brunner had regained his strength, he knew the decision could not be delayed any longer. They were all restless from inactivity and in the confined conditions of the burrow, tempers were starting to get short. Brunner was aware of all this and knew that it would be up to him as the new head of the family to make the choice.

So down there in the darkness, he listened to the others. Mataama was unhappy and openly chittered at her cubs in disagreement. Both of them were now almost independent of her in their own right. This left Brunner facing the unenviable task of deciding between two fundamentally opposed viewpoints.

Mataama did not want to leave the lake where she had lived for so many years, despite everything that had happened. It was her home. She had had her kits here. She wanted to get to the far end of the lake and build there.

Petwa and Chipwe, however, were adamant that as long as the men remained, no place on the lake would be safe. The men would find them and destroy them once and for all. They wanted to leave immediately and do what Brunner himself had done. They should all trek away and find a new lake or river far from the men and start afresh.

Brunner secretly agreed with them. There was no other realistic option. He also understood the instinct driving them to assert themselves like this. His problem was how to keep his new-found family together. It would be a cruel twist of fate if they were to split up now, so soon after he had been accepted by them. He had to find a way of reconciling Mataama to the inevitable before the others took matters into their own hands and weakened his authority.

Perhaps Mataama sensed this feeling in him with all its implications for herself. She became more agitated and kept leaving the little circle to disappear into the sleeping area for no apparent reason. She would return and interrupt them to fuss over unimportant details. She even tried to groom Petwa but he snapped at her and bared his teeth in anger. Chipwe also scolded her and Mataama backed away in alarm.

In the silence that followed, they all heard the sound of the crows drilling their beaks into the ground to summon them. From the noise, Brunner guessed that the entire flock had landed. Their tapping became more insistent. Brunner nudged Chipwe, who slipped down the burrow entrance and out into the lake.

The beavers waited, glad of the distraction. They strained to hear what was happening. Mataama began to clear the floor of tiny scraps of bark they had missed earlier. Petwa eventually went to help her. Brunner was bursting with impatience and finding it very hard not to go and find out what was happening for himself. A horrible thought struck him. Perhaps the men were coming back! They had located the burrow and even now were on their way to dig them out. His eyes flicked to the entrance hole in the floor. He could almost see Rufus's great head and jaws appearing. His pelt was suddenly damp with sweat. He knew Petwa was thinking the same. Where was Chipwe? Why was he wasting so much time?

Then they heard him whistling in excitement – or was it alarm? The next instant there was a loud splash, as if he had belly-flopped into the lake. They huddled close together, shivering in anticipation. There was a swirl of water in the entrance. It flooded across the floor of the chamber towards them and Chipwe's head shot up.

He came straight out of the water, shaking himself all over them and spluttering to get the news out.

'It's the men! The men! They're leaving! They're going away! The crows are following them.'

Brunner's heart lurched. Chipwe must have misheard or got it wrong. It couldn't be true. He had to know for himself.

Brunner raced after the crows like an animal possessed. It was true, the crows assured him with growing impatience at his slowness to understand. But now he did. Never had the air smelt so good or the grasses so sweet. The ground was a blur beneath his feet: the hot sunshine fragrant with the scents of summer.

Beside him, Mataama ran with an easy movement, the wound she had suffered in the explosion long since mended. Her eyes were suddenly bright and she blinked as they followed the crows circling ahead in the bright blue of the sky.

They splashed through a stream and impatiently tugged their feet clear of the sodden moss that seemed to delight in holding them back. Then they were scampering across an open space where heather and low clumps of blueberries grew. Above them, the crows called encouragement and laughed among themselves. The beavers followed with pounding hearts.

Brunner led the way up a long, rising slope to where a massive lichen-covered boulder lay half buried. It stood against the skyline like a tower. Here they stopped and flung themselves down on the short, springy turf. Below them, a steep bank fell away to the track the men had made. There were huge ruts and wheel marks to one side.

A hundred yards away, the track disappeared into the forest like a railway line entering a dark tunnel. The beavers whistled at each other in delight. The crows flew low overhead and told them to stay put and wait where they were. They flew away on lazy black wings to another part of the forest. Brunner found he could just make them out if he stood on tiptoe. He watched them circling round for what seemed an age. After a while, his eyelids drooped. It was just so wonderful to be out here in the light and feel the sun hot on one's face.

He woke with a start. Alarmed, he looked around to find the others fast asleep. Furious with himself for setting so bad an example, he ran across and nipped Chipwe's ear. His cry brought the others to their feet. Brunner scolded them but they knew he was far more angry with himself.

The crows seemed to have disappeared and for a horrible moment he wondered if they had misread the signs and that the men were not going after all. But even as he thought this, Mataama sat upright and hissed for them to be quiet. The crows were back. They were still some way away but even at that distance, Brunner could see they were behaving strangely. They were no longer circling. Instead they would dive towards the forest and then pull up into the sky to begin the manoeuvre all over again.

'They're attacking something,' said Chipwe, after they had watched for a while.

'The way hawks do,' Mataama agreed.

'I'm sure they're heading this way,' Petwa whistled.

He was right. The crows were growing bigger. Then, simultaneously, the beavers understood. Faintly, carried along on the playful breeze, they heard a sound that lifted the hair along their spines. It was a sound none of them could ever mistake. It was a low, grumbling noise which became charged with menace as it grew nearer. It grew louder. An ugly, greedy, tearing noise that meant only one thing – destruction.

Brunner sensed the others flinching from it and sidling round behind him. He swallowed, only to find his mouth had gone quite dry. He began to pant out loud through an open mouth. A porcupine appeared running down the track from the forest. Its spines were raised ready to defend itself against the oncoming monsters. As it emerged into the sunlight, it blinked and for a moment stood there peering from side to side until a loud clash of gears close behind sent it scuffling down towards the stream the beavers had crossed earlier, what now seemed to be an age ago.

The skin round Brunner's nose tightened as he felt the advancing tread of the machines through his paws. The crows were gathering like whirling leaves just above the tops of the trees, screaming defiance.

A huge yellow machine lurched out of the gloom. It came towards them, roaring its hatred of everything in its path. It belched black exhaust and a cloud of dust and flies swirled after it. A baleful yellow eye glared at them. It pulsed with malevolence.

Every hair on Brunner's body stood upright. He spat at the creature and went back a step and then another, only to find the boulder blocking any further retreat. He was aware of Mataama close by, but the younger ones must have run for cover.

The great beast came on, bellowing at him. There was that same hot stench and the clattering from its feet. It was slipping sideways over some loose sand. The crows were all round. They were landing beside him, holding their wings high against their bodies then jumping back into the air and swooping directly at the beast. There was a man on top of it. Brunner felt Mataama finally bolt. He was glad she had got away. She and her cubs would stay together now after this, he thought. They would build a new dam and live in peace.

The machine was level with him and he flinched, waiting for it to reach out and seize him. He saw the man with an arm raised to ward off the crows. Now there was nothing but noise and dust and fumes. It was impossible to see anything. Brunner put his head in his paws and rubbed at the grit in his eyes and nostrils. Perhaps the monster couldn't find him. Perhaps it was searching for him. There was another of them close by.

The roaring procession of machines seemed to stretch to infinity. Eventually the silence returned as suddenly as it had been broken. The hot swirling air cooled and settled and Brunner realised he could hear the squirrels scolding each other. The crows had left and were nowhere to be seen. There was just himself to tell the story and witness what he now realised was the men's retreat.

He eased himself away from the boulder and began to sneeze. When he had finished, he heard a whistle. He tried to reply but couldn't. He felt lightheaded. He had seen off the men and their terrible allies. He felt proud. The others would come back and find him. Let them.

He looked down the track where the monsters had fled. It was ripped, the ground torn open with their passing. The crows were starting to return. They swooped around him congratulating themselves and chuckling with glee. Mataama and Chipwe had joined him. Mataama was licking his face and Petwa was not far away.

Then something strange happened, strange even for that momentous afternoon. All of a sudden, a solitary jeep drove out of the forest and came bouncing along the track towards them. There was a man in the jeep and sitting beside him was a large dog. Brunner recognised them both at once. But it was the familiar sound of another dog barking that kept them all motionless.

Ranger came chasing after the vehicle, worrying at its rear wheels and running alongside hurling defiance at its occupants. As one, the beavers sprang up in rage. Brunner was aware of Mataama and the others alongside him, standing on their hind legs, spitting.

Ranger must have seen the movement because he suddenly raced past the jeep, which swung out and tried to hit him. The dog avoided it and scrambled up the slope to join the beavers. The crows took off with a great flapping of wings. Ranger stood beside Brunner barking like a mad thing as Bourassa and his dog drove past. Bourassa looked up, his mouth opening in surprise. He shook his fist at them. Then he was gone. But Rufus ... just looked away.

They watched the jeep drive out of their lives. A wonderful sense of relief gripped Brunner as he realised it was going to be all right now, for all of them.

Behind him, Ranger sat down, yawned and began to scratch.

POSTSCRIPT

From where it soared at 5,000 feet, the eagle could see almost one hundred miles. Behind it to the west, the mountains towered up in a colossal rampart, a natural barrier some hundreds of miles long which in parts was still unexplored. The snow lay thick on its peaks, dazzling in the bright summer sun.

It swung in a lazy spiral, head cocked to one side watching for any sudden flicker of movement below. Its talons clenched and then more slowly, opened. It sang to itself in a strange, joyless cry that neither rose nor fell but was whipped away to join the wind.

Where the mountains ended, a wilderness of lakes, scrub, fir trees and huge grey boulders stretched away to join the far horizon. The sun was reflected a million times in the stillness of the lake waters and a great peace covered the land.

Even the noise from a red helicopter failed to disturb the serenity. It seemed to disappear from view almost at once, swallowed up in the immensity of the landscape.

The great bird stared down. It noted the piles of earth recently levelled and the scars underneath. A dog was barking and running in and out of the trees chasing something, chipmunks probably. A man was bending over a boat at the water's edge.

The eagle felt a thermal pushing it upwards and lifted a massive wing to counter it. It slid down through the sky towards the lake beneath. As it descended, it noticed the slightest of disturbances in the water. A wake was spreading across the surface. Where it came to a point, the bird saw four small heads.

It circled, curious to find out more. The heads turned into a little river and continued swimming. At some point they must have dived. All the eagle saw were four rows of dancing bubbles and then they too were gone. The beavers had come home.